D0899383

The Trap

Brant was breathing hard, his face was cut and bloody, his eyes already swelling. As he lurched back a little farther, he glimpsed Pink Hanson's face once more. It was ablaze with exultation. His eyes glowed.

And in that fleeting glance, a blinding light of understanding struck Brant. With hair-trigger suddenness he realized the trap that had been set for him, into which he had so blindly walked. He saw now that he had been goaded into a wring he was bound to lose.

LONGHORN EMPIRE

Bradford Scott

LEISURE BOOKS NEW YORK CITY

A LEISURE BOOK®

January 2009

Published by special arrangement with Golden West Literary Agency.

Dorchester Publishing Co., Inc.
200 Madison Avenue
New York, NY 10016

ISBN 10: 0-8439-6152-X
ISBN 13: 978-0-8439-6152-2

LONGHORN EMPIRE

Chapter One

Old John Webb didn't know it, but he was looking upon the strengthening current of a flood that was to topple institutions, change history, influence the destiny of a nation and leave its indelible mark upon the habits, characteristics and ambitions of a people. The era in which Webb was taking a prominent part would in no great time disrupt his own orderly and contented life and bring turbulence to the vast domain wherein he was a veritable overlord with the powers and privileges of a feudal chieftain.

Young Austin Brant, with the greater vision of youth, sensed it dimly.

But at the moment it was not the destiny of nations that concerned Brant and Webb, but the condition of the Cimarron River only a few miles to the north. From the crest of the rise where they sat their horses, they could see on the trail below and some miles to the south, their great herd rolling northward, a sea of tossing horns and shaggy backs. Webb as owner and Brant as Trail Boss were anxious about the crossing they soon would have to attempt. If the Cimarron was on a rampage, and they had reason to believe it was, the crossing might be anything but easy. Already, the banks of the sinister river were well salted with the bones of cows, and of riders, who had risked the hazard of its turbulent waters.

The Cimarron was bad at all times. Even during most of the year when it was a sandy stretch with a small, sluggish current, it could be counted on to provide trouble. Its bed was full of treacherous quicksands which dragged down horses, cattle and men. Its channel was constantly shifting, and where yesterday there was a passable ford, today there might be a deep hole that was utterly unsuspected and which could easily mean disaster for the unwary.

From the crest of the rise, Webb and Brant could see the yellow torrent cutting the prairie like a giant rusty sword. They shook their heads in unison as they gazed upon it.

"Looks bad," remarked Webb.

"It does," agreed the Trail Boss, his glance shifting to the east.

"We might get held up," said Webb. "If we do, it means a big loss. I contracted to deliver this bunch by the eighth of the month, with a penalty for non-delivery."

Brant nodded. He didn't need to be told that. His gaze was still to the east, and his black brows drew together above the high bridge of the rather prominent nose between level gray eyes.

"Think we can risk it?" Webb persisted.

"Haven't made up my mind yet," Brant replied. "Want to get a closer look at that crik. Anyhow, I've a notion we'll find out whether it can be crossed or not. There's a big herd headed along the bank from the east. They'll hit Doran's Crossing before we get there. They're coming fast.

Look at the dust boil up! Whoever is handling that herd is either in a hurry or doesn't care how much fat he runs off his beefs."

"Sure looks that way," Webb returned absently. His glance shifted to the setting sun. "We had oughta be able to make it before dark, if we can make it at all," he said.

"Yes," agreed Brant. "There's better pasture on the far side."

"What's them shacks over there?" Webb asked.

"That's Doran," Brant replied. "That big one sprawled all over the flat is called Old Jane's Deadfall. It's a hell, all right. An old harridan named Jane Doran first set it up. The pueblo was named for her. She's gone, but the gents that later took over are saltier than she ever was. The place lives off the riders coming along this way, mostly with the drives."

Webb frowned. "And the boys will figger they're due a little bust, after ridin' this infernal river," he remarked.

Brant nodded sober agreement. "I'll keep an eye on them," he promised.

"And Cole Dawson in pertickler," Webb warned. "Cole is one of the best cowhands that ever came out of Texas, but put him in reach of a bottle and there's no tellin' what he'll do. Sometimes I wish I'd let him go. He ain't been right since I made you range boss of the Runnin' W. Cole figgered he'd get the job when Raines went into business on his own. He would have, if he hadn't such a hankerin' for red-eye."

"I've a notion he'll straighten out, sooner or later," Brant remarked.

Old John grunted, and looked far from convinced. Brant continued to eye the sky. Far to the west, above a range of low hills, a cloud was climbing, purple and piled, with an ominous flicker of lightning across its breast. The crests of the hills were swathed in violet mist, from which shot forth long, wavering streamers, akin to the banners of an advancing army. Brant shook his head dubiously.

"There's a bad storm under way over there," he told the Boss. "I sure don't like the looks of it."

"Don't 'pear to be comin' this way over fast," Webb commented.

"No," Brant agreed, "but something else is liable to come this way, and fast."

"What's that?"

"Water. A cloudburst up toward the head of the Cimarron sends water down the channel in big waves, and it sure raises hell. Comes almighty fast and sudden. We don't want to get caught by one with the cows in the middle of the river. But if we don't risk it and cross tonight, I got a feeling we won't get across for days. Come on, I want to see that herd ahead take the water."

The pair touched up their horses and rode swiftly down the sag. They proceeded across the prairie at a fast gallop, but before they reached the river bank, the herd from the east was already taking the water. The broad stream was crowded with shaggy heads and clashing horns as the cows streaked through the water like shooting stars bursting from a cloud bank. Bawling and blowing, the first steers made the far bank. And it was a long way off, for the Cimarron, often so shallow a man could wade it, was now a wild torrent swirling and roaring between its muddy banks.

Brant and Webb thrilled to the drama of the

crossing as they reined in a little distance to the last of the herd, which was pouring forward to take the water. Tensely they sat their horses, watching the tangled, bumping masses breast the current. Some went under, not to rise again. Calves were crushed and drowned. But the great body of the herd reached the solid ground of the far shore, shook the water from their hides and fell to grazing.

Glancing about, Austin Brant saw a man sitting his horse, motionless as a statue, a little to the right.

It was the horse that first held Brant's attention. Full seventeen hands high, it was a splendid bay with coal-black mane and tail. As fine a horse, almost, as Smoke, Brant's great blue moros. Speed, endurance, good nature, all were there, without a doubt.

But a single glance at the rider was enough to transfer his interest to the animal's owner. He was a tall man and slender, with the steely slenderness of a rapier blade. His eyes were intensely black, with a glitter to them like to knife points in the sun. His face, cameo-like in its regularity of feature, had a healthy outdoor look, but the skin was the type that tans but little no matter how much exposed to wind and sun. The paleness of complexion was less startling in contrast to his dark eyes than was his hair, a crisply golden mane curling down almost to his collar. All in all, there was a restless, untamed look to the motionless horsemen sitting lance-straight under the darkening sky. Austin Brant fell it, and felt also the magnetic personality that dwelt beneath the unbelievably handsome face and perfect form.

"So damn good looking it hurts!" he muttered. "And a hell raiser if there ever was one. Salty, with plenty of wrinkles on his horns. Wonder who he is?"

The tall stranger filled that lack a moment later. He noted Brant's gaze upon him, flashed a smile and rode over to greet the new arrivals.

"Kane's the handle," he introduced, extending a slim, capable looking hand. "Norman Kane."

Brant and Webb supplied their own names and shook hands gravely.

"See your critters wear a Flyin' V burn," the latter remarked, by the way of making conversation.

"Yes, that's my brand," Kane replied. "My spread's over to the southeast of here."

"Good range?"

"Could be better," Kane answered, his brows drawing together slightly. "Fact is, I've about decided to pull up stakes and move farther west. Grass isn't what it should be, and there's very little shelter against bad weather. I prefer a hill range, where there are canyons and coulees for the critters to hole up against storms and too much sun."

"That's right," agreed Webb. "Nothin' like it. I got plenty of hills down in the Texas Panhandle. Good grass, too, and enough water."

Kane nodded, his eyes thoughtful.

"My brand's Runnin' W, startin' sort of like yours, but twice over," Webb supplied.

"And I notice your herd is about twice mine, too," Kane chuckled, flashing a smile. "Figger to take the water?"

"It's up to Brant," Webb replied, jerking his thumb toward his foreman. "I'm follerin' his lead. He's been here before."

Brant's eyes were again on the ominous western sky. The cloud bank had climbed little higher, but was thicker and darker than before. The hill crests were totally obscured now by the drifting rain mists which the wind whipped into fantastic shapes illuminated by the fitful lightning glare.

"Haven't made up my mind yet," he told Kane. "Sure don't like the looks of the weather over there."

"If you don't make it this evenin' you're liable to get stuck here for several days," Kane observed.

"I'm taking that into account," Brant replied. "We can't afford to get stuck, but we can afford less to lose our cows in a sudden flood."

"It would hardly come down that fast," said Kane.

Austin Brant turned his level gray graze upon the other's face.

"Ever make this drive before?" he questioned. Kane shook his handsome head.

"Nope, I never did," he admitted. "But I've rode other rivers."

"The Cimarron is in a class by itself," Brant returned grimly. "But we'll see. Here come the cows."

"And here comes Cole Dawson for his powders," Webb said.

A moment later Dawson pulled rein beside the group.

"Well," he rumbled, "all set to hit the wet?"

Brant did not answer immediately. He seemed to look the cowboy over speculatively.

Cole Dawson was worth looking at. He was a giant of a man, more than six feet in height, tall almost as Austin Brant, and pounds heavier. His shoulders were thick and slightly bowed. His great hairy hands were affixed to powerful corded wrists and when Dawson was standing on his trunk-like legs, they dangled nearly to his knees. He had a bad-tempered face dominated by hot blue eyes. His lips were thick, but firmly set, his nose fleshy and bulbous. He looked what he was, a hard man but a capable one.

"Well," he repeated, "all set to go?"

Brant turned his gaze back to the west, and still hesitated. A sneer writhed Dawson's thick lips, showing his stubby, tobacco-stained teeth.

"Scairt of a puddle of water?" he jeered.

"Any fool can get a herd, and himself, drowned," Brant returned quietly.

Dawson's face flushed darkly red. He opened his lips to reply, but old John Webb cut him short.

"Be enough of this," said the Running W owner. "I got enough troubles without you two young roosters spurrin' each other. We're here to get this herd to Dodge City, not to argify. Brant has the say, and what he says goes."

Dawson shut up. When old John spoke in that tone of voice, he expected, and usually got, obedience. If he didn't get it, the jigger he spoke to got something *he* didn't like.

On Norman Kane's classically handsome face was a faintly amused smile, but his eyes held a speculative gleam as they rested on the angry Dawson.

Austin Brant abruptly made up his mind. "All right," he snapped, "we'll risk it. Get 'em moving, Dawson. The logs tied fast to the chuck wagons? Okay, we'll float them across first. They wouldn't have a chance if the water came down suddenly.

Have two hands rope to each wagon to help the horses. And four or five of the boys standing on the upstream side of each one, against an overturn. Others can lead their horses across. Let's go."

With work to do, private feuds were instantly forgotten. Dawson wheeled his horse and rode back to meet the herd and relay the Trail Boss' orders. Within fifteen minutes the two wagons, each with a big cottonwood log lashed on either side, hit the water. Several times before they reached the far bank it looked bad, but largely due to Dawson's skill in handling the chore, they got across safely. Dawson and his hands, including those who had steadied the wagons and mounted the horses led across for them, returned to the near bank.

"Now for it," said Brant. "In they go. Thank the Lord the bank is low here and over there, so we don't have to make dugways."

He gave a last glance into the ominous west. He could see less than a mile along the course of the river now, because of the mists that were thickening over the water.

The yelling cowboys sent the cattle into the river with a rush. The cows didn't want to go, but they went. At first they sloshed through the shallows, bellowing complaints. A moment later, however, they were swimming. Brant, sitting his horse at the water's edge, watched with a darkening face.

"She's getting higher by the minute," he told Webb. "I don't like it, but maybe we'll pull through."

Cole Dawson was working like a demon. His roaring voice sounded loud above the turmoil as he cursed the cows, the river and the hands. From time to time he darted a sneering glance at Austin Brant. As the last of the herd bawl-bellered into the water, he sent his horse plunging for the river.

"That feller's got nerve," observed Norman Kane, who had remained on the hither side of the river to watch the Running W cows take the water. "He—hell and blazes!"

Brant and Webb followed his staring eyes and swore in turn. Less than a quarter of a mile upstream, racing through the swirling mists, was a solid wall of water a full ten feet in height. Its tossing crest was speckled with uprooted trees and bushes. Roaring, thundering, it hurtled downstream.

Rigid with suspense, the three men on the river bank watched it come. Brant's gaze flickered toward the rear of the herd. The cows were two-thirds of the way across, sensing their danger and swimming frantically for safety. Well in the rear was Cole Dawson. He had slipped from his saddle and was swimming beside his horse, clinging with one hand to the horn. They could see him roar encouragement to the men in front, but no sound came to them above the tumult of the rushing waters.

Dawson abruptly realized his danger. He twisted his face about to glare upstream. Then he redoubled his efforts. But he was hundreds of yards from the far bank and safety when the thundering wall of water overtook him. Old John let out a yell of horror—

"That cottonwood's got him! He's under!"

Dawson had vanished in a welter of foam and

tossing branches as the uprooted tree swept him beneath the surface. His horse barely cleared the thrashing branches and diagonalled toward the shore.

"Look!" roared Kane. "Look! There he comes! He's wedged in a fork!"

Dawson's limp body had reappeared, jammed in the V formed by two great branches. The three rolled in the wake of the wave crest. Dawson vanished once more.

Old John yelled again. "Where you goin', you loco idiot!" he bellowed at Austin Brant. But even as he spoke, Smoke was racing downstream toward where the river curved, with an eddy washing back toward the near bank.

Like a scud of blue fog on the wings of a gale, the great moros raced downstream. He reached the bend ahead of the tumbling wave. The tree that had been Dawson's undoing was considerably back of the crest now, and by some freak of chance had ceased to roll. It still hurtled downstream, but Dawson's flaccid form shone clear of the water.

"It's liable to start rollin' again any minute, though," gulped Webb.

"That feller's got a head on him," Kane exclaimed as Brant slid from the saddle and ran to the lip of the high bank overlooking the bend. "He figgered the eddy will jerk the tree in close to the bank where mebbe he can reach Dawson. Come on, let's get down there."

Together they urged their horses toward the bend. Kane swore excitedly as the tree swung in toward the bank and Austin Brant crouched on the crumbling edge.

"He's goin' to jump to the tree!" Kane yelped. "Hell, what a chance he's takin'! If that trunk starts rollin' again when he lands on it, it'll be curtains for 'em both. There he goes!"

The tree had swung in to within a few yards of the bank. Before it could eddy out again, Brant launched his long body through the air in a prodigious spring. The riders gasped in unison as the trunk surged beneath the water under the impact of his weight.

Brant landed within arm's reach of Dawson's helpless body. He teetered precariously for an instant, caught his balance and edged along the almost submerged trunk. Webb and Kane saw the log begin to slowly turn again as it swerved away from the shore in the grip of the eddy. Brant clutched Dawson's collar with both hands, heaved mightily. The crotch held the body firmly and refused to let go. Kane and Webb saw him shift the grip of one hand, fumble with Dawson's belt.

"The feller's gun and holster are caught on a snag!" barked Kane. "He's got it loose! There they go into the water!" He had plucked his rope free and was twirling a loop as he spoke. As they raced up to the bend, Dawson and Brant broke surface, the range boss still gripping Dawson's collar. He turned sideways and began to swim strongly toward the shore.

"Catch!" roared Kane, sliding to the ground and snaking his loop. He sent the rope hissing through the air. The loop fell almost over Brant's extended hand. He seized it and twisted the rope about his arm.

"Give a hand!" Kane barked to Webb. Together they hauled in with all their strength. The eddy tore at the two forms with gripping fingers, but Brant fought strongly against the watery pull. Kane and Webb whirled about and walked away from the bank, the taut rope humming over their shoulders. Another moment of mighty struggle and the half drowned Trail Boss and his helpless burden were dragged onto the steep slope of the bank. Kane leaped down to assist Brant. Together they levered Dawson's bulky form up until old John, lying flat and reaching down, could get a grip on Dawson's collar. The rest was easy. A moment more and Dawson lay sprawled on the prairie, Austin Brant crawled to safety and lay panting beside him.

Old John removed his hat and mopped his damp brow. Norman Kane grinned down at the prostrate pair.

"A plumb fine chore," he told Brant. "Feller, you'll do for any man to ride the river with!"

Brant grinned back, rather wanly. "Reckon if it wasn't for quick thinking on your part, we'd both be a long ways down, and underneath, by now," he declared.

Cole Dawson was groaning and retching with returning consciousness. He opened his eyes, raised himself on his elbow and for a minute was frankly sick. Muttering an oath, he sat up and glared at the group.

"Who drug me out?" he demanded thickly.

"Well, I don't see but one gent with wet clothes," rumbled Webb, nodding toward Austin Brant who was rising to his feet.

Dawson glowered up at the Trail Boss. "It would hafta be him!" he growled.

"Why, you ungrateful—" old John began, but

Brant snapped, "Hold it!" and Webb closed his lips on the uncompleted sentence. Norman Kane regarded the scene with his enigmatical smile and said nothing.

"Well," observed Brant, "that river looks pretty bad, but the big run the cloudburst over west set off looks to have passed. Think we can risk it?"

"I believe we can," Kane replied. "But what about Dawson? His horse is on the other side."

"Don't you worry about Dawson," spat that individual, shaking himself like a great dog. "I can hang on to the Boss' stirrup and get there as easy as the rest of you. Let's go."

"Okay," agreed Webb, "let's take it before another loose ocean comes down that infernal crik."

Before they reached the opposite bank, Austin Brant was of the opinion more than once that their day of death by drowning was at hand. But reach it they did, pretty well exhausted, but suffering no more serious consequences. The giant Dawson, despite a knot the size of a hen's egg on his head appeared to be in as good shape as anybody else. Without a word to anybody he stamped off to see to the bedding down of the herd.

"If he ain't the limit!" snorted old John. Austin Brant shrugged his broad shoulders. Norman Kane smiled.

Chapter Two

After a change to dry clothing, Brant felt ready for anything. As he combed his thick black hair, he reflected on the singular character of Cole Dawson. His thoughts shifted to Norman Kane and he shook his head.

"Cool as a dead snake," he told himself, apropos of the Flying V owner. " 'Peared to look on the whole business as a joke. I've a notion he looks on most everything as a joke. That is," he added reflectively, "if the joke doesn't happen to be on him. If it is, I've a notion it isn't over nice for the joker."

Brant chose his hands carefully for night guard duty—killpecker, graveyard, dead-hour, wake-up and cocktail. He picked the oldest and steadiest men for the various chores.

"The rest of you can head for the Deadfall, like you're itching to, as soon as we eat," he told the others; "but watch your step. We're trailing out of here come daylight, headaches or no headaches, and I dont want to catch a man in a shape he can't fork his saddle."

The cowboys grinned at him, but just the same they knew he meant what he said.

After supper was over, Brant conferred with Webb. "I'm sort of tuckered," old John admitted.

"Swimmin' that river wasn't so good, at my age, but there's nothin' wrong a good night's sleep won't take care of. If you feel up to takin' charge by yourself, I'll head for a mite of shuteye."

"Go to it," Brant told him. "I'm all set for anything. You start pounding your ear pronto. Nothing to worry about. We lost some cows today, but not too many. We're all set."

Outside the wagon where Webb was bedding down, Brant paused to roll a cigarette. The night was pitch black, the sky heavily overcast, except when fitful lightning flashes cast an eerie glow across the prairie. Occasional plumps of rain drummed the wagon canvas. A wailing wind bent the grass heads and echoed occasional low rumbles of thunder.

Brant glanced toward the rambling bulk of the Deadfall. It appeared like a handful of fallen stars because of the light within shining through the chinks between the logs. Through the open windows came the sounds of revelry and mirth, growing louder as the night progressed. Brant shook his head, and his eyes narrowed slightly with concern.

"If there isn't trouble before this night is over, I'm a heap mistaken," he predicted gloomily. He pinched out his cigarette, tossed the butt aside and headed for the building.

When Brant stepped inside the big main room of the place, he was blinded by the glare of light within. The numerous hanging and bracket lamps were fed with oil from boiled-down buffalo fat, and that commodity was still plentiful on the Cimarron Trail. His vision quickly cleared, however, and he glanced about with interest.

The room was a singular combination of frontier crudeness and civilized garishness. Homemade tables and chairs vied with plate glass mirrors for attention. The floor was of puncheon boards, the log walls not even whitewashed, but on those walls hung oil paintings. The long bar was constructed of rough planks, while the backbar, adorned with the out-of-place mirrors, was pyramided with bottles of every color and shape.

Not for a moment did Brant believe that the "luxuries" had all been imported from the east at prodigious expense.

"More than one wagon train has come up short in those parts," he shrewdly deduced. "This diggin' was furnished by robbery and it exists chiefly by robbery, or I'm making a big mistake."

The room was crowded, for several outfits returning from northern drives were stopping off at the crossing. The occupants were chiefly cowhands, but there was a sprinkling of hardeyed individuals whose hands, Brant felt sure, bore no marks of rope or branding iron.

They were the "camp followers" of the drives, assembled at Doran's for the purpose of preying on the cowhands in one way or another. Brant spotted more than one occupying places at the poker tables with stacks of gold pieces before them.

"Taking the boys over, all right," he muttered. "Well, they'd better lay off my bunch if they know what's good for them."

Mechanically, he shifted his heavy guns in their carefully cut-out holsters a little higher about his lean waist.

Lounging at the far end of the bar was a big black-bearded man who masked with a bluff manner and an attitude of jovial goodfellowship the temper and disposition of a Gila Monster. Brant knew he called himself Phil Doran and claimed to be the nephew of old Jane who opened the place. Beside him stood a younger and slighter man with a sallow, wedge-shaped faced and red-rimmed beady eyes set very close together. It was Pink Hanson, Doran's partner. The unsavory pair owned the Deadfall.

Seated at a nearby table were Norman Kane and Cole Dawson, engaged in earnest conversation. Brant's black brows drew together as he speculated the pair. Kane, without looking up, leaned closer and said somthing in low tones to his companion. A moment later Dawson got to his feet and slouched to the bar.

"Saw me come in and decided to break it up," Brant told himself. "Now what's building between those two?"

The two occupants of another table near the wall, upon which rested dishes of food, caught Brant's attention. One was a lean, grizzled, elderly man with a lined face, a tight mouth and tufted brows. He had the look of a hard man. The other occupant of the table was a big-eyed girl who couldn't have been more than twenty at the outside. She had short, soft brown hair, inclined to curl, a red mouth and a small but well rounded figure. She appeared to be intensely interested in what went on around her, and rather bewildered.

Brant felt a sense of disapproval that amounted to indignation.

"The devil of a place to bring a nice woman," he muttered, eyeing the elderly man with decided disapproval.

But the obvious explanation of her presence quickly came to him. After all, the Deadfall was the only place near the crossing where anything decent to eat could be obtained.

"And that old jigger with her looks able to take care of himself, and her," he decided. "Her Dad, I reckon."

He sauntered to the bar, found a vacant place and ordered a drink. Turning, he swept the room with his glance. He quickly spotted a group of his own hands at a table, glasses beside them, playing poker. As he watched, one shrugged his shoulders, got to his feet and headed for the bar. Instantly a man standing nearby slid into the vacant chair. The other players glanced at him questioningly, but the dealer muttered something and they settled back into their seats.

Austin Brant left the bar and strode across the room. He tapped the man on the shoulder.

"I don't care to have my hands play with strangers when they're on a drive," he said.

The man, a big, beefy individual, snarled up at him like a rat.

"You keep your nose out of my business, high-pockets, if you know what's good for you," he spat.

"You heard what I said," Brant replied. "Get out of that chair."

The man got out, his eyes glaring, his fists doubled. Brant hit him, left and right, hard. He shot through the air and landed on the floor with a crash. He rolled over and scrambled to his feet, blood and curses pouring from his mouth. His hand shot down. Then he froze in a grotesquely strained position. He was looking into the muzzle of two long black guns.

"Don't—try—it," Brant advised, spacing the words.

Doran came rushing across the room. The muzzle of Brant's gun shifted the merest trifle.

"Goes for you, too, Doran," he said quietly.

Doran, who never forgot a face, recognized the Running W foreman from his previous visit to the Deadfall.

"Why, hello, Brant," he called jovially. "Just wanted to see what was goin' on. It's my business to keep order, you know."

He turned to the other man.

"You get up to the end of the bar and stay there, Porter," he directed. "You're lucky you didn't get your insides blowed out. This feller is as pizen with a gun as he is with his fists. Get goin'!"

The other started to bawl a protest, but something he saw in Doran's eyes evidently changed his mind for him. He clamped his bloody lips shut, turned and slouched away. Doran nodded affably to Brant and resumed his place at the lower end of the bar.

Brant holstered his guns, smiled at his grinning hands, and returned to his unfinished drink. As he passed the table occupied by the girl and the old man he glanced in their direction. The girl's eyes were wider than before, and there was a hint of something like terror in them as they rested upon the Running W foreman. Brant flushed slightly, and turned his back.

"Reckon she's got me down for one of the killer pack she's been told about," he growled under his breath. "Well, what the hell difference does it make to me!"

Chapter Three

The incident between Brant and the ambitious tinhorn seemed to have an exhilarating effect on the gathering in the Deadfall. Voices grew louder and more raucous. The fiddlers back of the dance floor sawed more vigorously. The dancers whirled with a wilder abandon. Even the roulette wheels developed a sharper clirk and whir. Somebody started bawling what was intended for song. Others took it up and the hanging lamps flickered to the din. Brant shook his head as the hectic hours passed.

"Trouble in the making," he declared to himself. "It'll bust loose any minute."

Trouble did bust loose, and Cole Dawson started it. The Running W poker game had fizzled out from lack of competition. The losers borrowed back from the winners and the players joined their companions at the bar. They mingled with the punchers of a returning outfit, the Tree L. Dawson and a lanky Tree L hand got to discussing brands and their altering. The argument grew heated. Suddenly, with a bellow of anger, Dawson knocked the other down. One of the cowboy's companions hurled Dawson sideways against the bar with a swinging blow. A Running W hand sent Dawson's attacker off his feet with a hard punch to the mouth. Another Tree L waddie returned the compliment, and there were three men on the floor. Instantly the whole section of the bar was a hitting, wrestling, cursing tangle. The barkeeps howled to stop it. Doran and Pink Hanson uttered soothing yells and tried to pull the battlers apart. Chairs and tables went over splintering and crashing. The dance floor girls screamed. The dealers and floor men bellowed for order, and didn't get it. Folks who really weren't concerned in the row got hit by accident and immediately became enthusiastic participants. The whole room boiled and seethed like a giant pot.

Austin Brant streamed across the room, dived into the mess and got Cole Dawson by the collar. He jerked him back out of the shindig. Dawson writhed around in Brant's grasp, roared a string of cuss words and swung a blow at the foreman. Before it had travelled six inches it was blocked. Brant whirled Dawson about and levered his arm behind his back and up between his shoulder blades. He ran Dawson on tiptoe through the door.

"I'll bust your arm for you, Cole, if you don't behave," he warned. "What's the matter with you, anyhow? You know we got work to do. The Old Man would hand you your time if I told him about this. Now head for camp and sober up. You can raise all the hell you want when we get to Dodge and turn over the herd. Now get going."

Rather to Brant's surprise, Dawson obeyed

orders. When Brant released his arm, he lurched off through the darkness, mumbling and muttering.

Brant returned to the saloon. Doran and Hanson and the floor men had managed to restore order. There were some bloody noses and discoloring eyes, but no serious damage had been done. Brant saw Norman Kane still sitting at his table, smiling his thin, cynical smile. He glanced toward where the girl and the old man sat. The girl was hunched back in her chair, her red lips slightly parted, her face rather white. The oldster was unconcernedly stuffing black tobacco into a blacker pipe. Brant walked over to the table.

"Not exactly the place for a lady, suh," he remarked pointedly.

The old man nodded. "Reckon you're right, son," he agreed without rancor. "Sort of new and rambunctious for my little niece here—she's from back East—but I don't pay it no mind. I've seen the elephant before."

"How come you to be in this section?" Brant asked curiously.

"We're just passin' through," the other replied. "We're headin' for the Texas Panhandle country. Our wagons are over east of the ford."

"What part of the Panhandle?" Brant asked with interest.

"South Canadian River country," the other said. "Town near where I got title to a spread is call Tascosa. The spread, the Bar O, is about twenty miles to the northwest."

"I remember it. Used to belong to old Clifton Taylor," Brant remarked.

"That's right. Taylor came back to Oklahoma,

where he was brought up. I made a deal with him. Traded my holdings in Oklahoma and some hard money for his Texas outfit."

"You'll sort of be neighbors to the Running W, the outfit I work for," Brant observed. "We range to the south and west of the Bar O."

"That's nice," said the oldster. "Be glad to know somebody in a new section. My name's Loring, Nate Loring. My niece's name is Verna Loring. Her Dad was my younger brother. Went East and died there last year."

Brant uspplied his own name and they shook hands. Verna glanced up rather timidly through the silken veil of her long lashes, but gave him a slim little hand. Apparently some of her fear was evaporating.

Old Nate stood up. "Well," he said, "reckon we'll be moseyin' along. Want to get an early start in the mornin', if that dadblamed river behaves. Hope to see you down in Texas, son."

"You will," Brant promised emphatically. "We'll be glad to have you for neighbors and we'll send over some of the boys to help you get located as soon as we get back from the drive. Yes, I'll be seeing you."

Old Nate nodded, and headed for the door, Verna swaying gracefully beside him. At the door she glanced back for an instant, her blue eyes met Brant's gray ones, held. She turned quickly and vanished into the night.

Austin Brant drew a deep breath. He glanced around at a sound and saw Norman Kane at his elbow. Kane was staring toward the door, the glitter in his black eyes intensified.

"You see interesting things in this hangout," he remarked.

"Uh-huh," Brant agreed absently, "you do."

The first beams of the rising sun found the Running W trail herd streaming north. Some distance ahead was a dust cloud that marked Norman Kane's Flying V critters, which had gotten under way first. Still farther ahead another cloud denoted a herd that came from north of the Cimarron to hit the Dodge City trail.

To the west and south a third cloud spotted still another outfit rolling in behind the Running W. The longhorns were on the march, as they had been for nearly ten years, as they would be for close to another decade, in the course of which they would change the face of the land, the habits of the people, and the aims and history of the West.

Nothing could stop the onward march of the long-horns. Cholera, Spanish fever, swollen rivers and other difficulties of the trail, loss of riders and loss of cows, rifles in the hands of angry grangers, prohibitory laws—all made the attempt, but the horns continued to clash, the wild eyes to roll, the shaggy backs heave, with the north and the towns of the north ever in view. The territories were filling up with land seekers who needed untold thousands of cattle to stock their ranges. The cities and the towns demanded cheap meat. Boom towns like Virginia City, Gold Hill and Deadwood were willing to pay any price for it. The government needed millions of pounds for the Indians herded onto the reservations and no longer able to supply their needs from the buffalo.

All these provided the necessary incentive for the great drives that began on the watersheds of the Brazos, the Colorado, the far-off Nueces and the mysterious Pecos and thundered north. There was a golden harvest to be reaped. The cattle owners, large and small, were out to get their share. Nothing should stop them. Nothing could stop them. The great barons of the open range lived like feudal lords on this golden flood. Small owners and individual cowboys sensed opportunity. The herds grew, the drivers became larger, more frequent. The bawling of worried cows, the blatting of frightened calfs, the rumblings of disgruntled steers rose with the cursing, the song, the crack of six-shooters and the shouting of orders in a pandemonium that disturbed the silence of nature from the Gulf to Kansas, and beyond.

It was the wild, unordered, triumphant song of marching empire. Born of economic necessity plus the challenge of the wilderness, the vast migration brought a dozen great states into being, made of Chicago the granary of the world and left an impress that would be plain half a century later, and more. The march of the Texas longhorns! The saga of the individualist! The very spirit of America laughing at the wilderness, setting to naught the problems of distance and terrain, accelerating the wheels of progress, creating a legend, a literature, turning dreams into realities and merging the impossible with the possible in a common pattern of fact.

Twenty to twenty-five miles a day were covered in the early days of a drive, so that the cows were tired when night came and less liable to stampede. Later this was cut down to an average of more like ten. But with Dodge City still some seventy miles distant, Austin Brant stepped up the speed of the drive until the cows were travelling nearly as fast as they did when started north across the Texas Panhandle.

"It's gettin' close to our deadline date," Webb had told him when they left the crossing. "If things go along smooth, we're okay, but if somethin' should happen to delay us, the loop will be drawn mighty tight."

So Brant took no chances and pushed the herd along at top speed.

"Looks like Norman Kane has a deadline to meet, too," he observed to Webb on the morning of the second day from Doran's Crossing. "He's keeping ahead of us right along."

"Uh-huh, it does look that way," Webb agreed. "I've a notion that young feller is a mighty smart cowman, Austin, and a sort of cold proposition along with it."

"I figure you're right on both counts," Brant nodded. "He's the sort of jigger who makes a first class general when a war busts loose."

"Uh-huh, and when things bust loose wrong, the sort that makes a fust class—anything," old John predicted. "I wouldn't want to get tangled up with him. I've a hunch he would take any short cut that worked well for him."

"Mebbe," Brant temporized, "but I've a notion he's got too cool a head to go off half-cocked."

Old John grunted, but made no further comment.

Scouting far in advance, Brant looked back at the moving mass of cattle, spread out like a great arrowhead, the point to the front, the base more than a mile wide. It was a big herd, even for those days, nearly three thousand head. Brant had twenty cowhands riding the herd, some six or seven more than the usual number for a herd that size. He was taking no chances.

There had been trouble a-plenty on the trail to Dodge City. The great herds afforded fat pickings for ruthless and daring bands that would swoop down on the bedded cattle at night, stampede them and cut out a sizeable bunch that they would run into some hidden canyon or gorge. The wrathful cowboys would be too busy for some time getting their scattered charges together to attempt pursuit, and even after the cows were rounded up and quieted once more, they did not dare leave them unguarded. Knowing this, Brant had made a plan which he hoped would foil any attempt on the Running W herd. For it he needed extra men. So far, except for the mishap at the Cimarron crossing, the drive had been singularly uneventful.

"Too darn easy," Brant told himself. "I got a feeling something is liable to bust loose. Sure wish we were at Dodge City."

He rode to the crest of a rise and glanced back. Everything looked to be in perfect order. The herd was rolling forward at a good pace. The hands were in their proper places. Near the head of the lumbering column and a little to each side were the point or lead men. This was the position of greatest responsibility, for it was they who must determine the exact direction taken. When it was desirable to veer the herd, the point man on one side would ride in toward the cattle, while his partner on the other side would edge away.

The cows would swerve away from the approaching horseman and toward the one that was moving away from them.

About a third of the way back were the swing riders, where the herd would begin to bend in case of a change of course. Another third back rode the flank riders. It was their duty to assist the swing riders in preventing the cows from wandering sidewise, and to drive off any stray cattle from other outfits joining up with the marching herd.

Last of all, cursing the dust and the poky and obstinate critters that always drift to the rear, came the drag or tail riders. This is the most disagreeable chore of the trail, but on this particular drive, Brant had chosen his drag men with the utmost care, for he was taking no chances on a sudden foray on a lagging portion of the herd. Cole Dawson, alert, vigilant, and capable had the drag riders and the rear of the herd under his personal supervision. Some distance back was the remuda of spare horses.

Following up the remuda came the two lumbering chuck wagons, the drivers sitting with Winchester rifles ready to hand. As the day drew to a close, the wagons would speed up and pass around the herd, so that the cooks could get busy at the camping site chosen by the Trail Boss and have supper ready by the time the herd was bedded down for the night.

A mile or so west of the trail was a range of low hills, their slopes covered with dense growth. The growth straggled out onto the prairie in a shadowy tangle. Suddenly Brant's eyes caught a gleam amid the bristle, as of reflected sunlight on shifted metal. A moment later he saw it again. His brows drew together and he tensed in his hull. He sent Smoke down the sag at a slow pace. Apparently he was facing to the front, but his slanted eyes studied the dark tangle at the base of the hills. A third time he sighted the tell-tale gleam, and once, where the growth thinned somewhat, he was sure he sensed movement amid the chaparral.

"There's a hellion over there riding herd on us, sure as shooting," he growled. "I don't like the looks of this."

As evening drew near, Brant grew anxious about a bedding-down site for the herd. They were passing over an exceedingly dry stretch of prairie. Not since morning had he encountered a stream or a spring. He knew that by now the cows must be badly in need of water. From time to time he could hear the querulous bleating of the tired and thirsty critters as they slogged wearily across the prairie.

Gradually the ground became more broken, with long rises, isolated clumps of rocks and occasional beetling cliffs. The sun was low in the overcast sky when Brant noticed, a few miles ahead, a silvery gleam winding out of the northwest. He drew a deep breath of relief. It was a small stream cutting across the route the cattle followed. A little later and Smoke had his nose buried in the cool water.

Brant traced the course of the stream with his eyes. He saw that it flowed from the dark mouth of a narrow canyon that slashed the hills about a mile to the north. He eyed the opening with interest. So far as he could see, it was the only break in the wall of the hills anywhere near. He glanced swiftly to the west, and again he thought he sighted movement in the fringe of brush. His lips set in a hard line. He turned his attention to the immediate terrain.

Across the stream was a stretch of level grass land that rolled to the foot of a wide cliff that based a fairly high rise. A few hundred yards from the foot of the cliff a gentle slope began. It terminated in a bench perhaps a score of yards wide. Then came a slight slope to a second and narrower bench that shouldered against the upward loom of the cliff. Brant nodded with satisfaction, turned in his saddle and again studied the canyon mouth. The second bench curved around the stand of cliffs and sloped downward to the prairie floor. From there on was open prairie to the canyon mouth, with the stream cutting across it in a series of curves.

Glancing back, Brant saw the chuck wagons had forged ahead and were rolling toward him at no great distance to the rear. He waved them to come on and set about deciding the best place for the camp.

Bedding down a herd was no snide chore. The critters must not be crowded too closely. Neither should they be scattered over too much ground. Brant knew that, well grazed and watered, the herd would lie quietly about half the night. Then, just as if a signal had been given by some leader, the cows would get on their feet, stretch, yawn, amble about a step or two. After a few grunts and rumbles, they would lie down again, generally on the other side. Just sort of like a cowpoke sitting up in his blankets to roll and smoke a cigarette then turning over and snuggling back to rest.

The cows would be allowed to drift from the bed ground as soon as day dawned. The cocktail riders, the last of the night guard shift, would move them in the right direction before the day herders took over and the weary night men hustled to surround their morning chuck.

"Unhitch up on that first bench and make camp there," Brant told the chuck wagon drivers. "Good place to cook and eat."

"Good for sleepin', too," observed one of the drivers. "Nice soft grass and enough of a cliff overhang to cut off the wind and most of the rain if it happens to cut loose durin' the night. Better shelter up on that second bench, but the ground under the cliff looks almighty hard and rocky."

Brant nodded, but did not comment.

Soon the herd came bawl-bellerin' up to the stream. The cows drank prodigiously, then began grazing on the rich grass. Brant sat his horse and watched them for some minutes. Occasionally, his gaze, grown contemplative, would shift across the prairie toward the dark canyon mouth from which the stream rolled like a tarnished silver ribbon. He glanced at the darkening sky, shook his head and rode up to the bench where the cooks were busy with their skillets and ovens.

After supper was over and the night guards posted, Brant gave some orders that caused his men to stare.

"Leave your bedrolls down here by the fire," he told them. "Each of you take a couple of blankets and bed down on that second bench, close to the cliff. Everybody sleeps in his clothes tonight—everything, including boots and guns. The horses are to be tied up there, too, under full rig." He called six men by name.

"You jiggers bed down over here with me," he directed. "All right, you better hit the hay. May not get much shuteye tonight, can't tell."

The hands grumbled and swore, but did as directed. On a drive the word of the Trail Boss is law. Not even the owner questions his orders. All responsibility is his, and in consequence, all authority.

John Webb drew Brant aside. "You figger there might be trouble tonight, Austin?" he asked.

"Could be," Brant replied.

"You figger somebody might make a try for our cows?"

"Could be," Brant repeated. "I'm playing a hunch, that's all. If it's a fool hunch, there isn't much damage done, aside from considerable cussin', but if it turns out to be a straight one, well, you might be glad I sort of took precautions."

"Your chore," grunted old John, with a shrug of his big shoulders.

"So I figure," Brant returned. "Now I'm going to ride down for a gab with the night hawks."

"Be a fine night for any hellions with notions," Webb growled. "So dark you can't see twenty feet, and the wind kickin' up enough row to drown any noise, and enough rain mist to deaden sounds, too."

Brant rode down to the level prairie, circled the herd and talked to each night hawk in turn.

"Keep back in the shadow," he told them. "There's no thunder or lightning, and no signs of any, and just enough wind and rain to keep the critters bunched for warmth. They should be plumb quiet all night, unless something sets them off. If something does, don't ride in to the herd. Ride away from it, and ride out a good piece, pull up and be all set to start 'em millin' if they scatter. Don't forget what I told you, now, or you're liable to pay heavy for the mistake."

He rode back to the bench, leaving the night guards considerably mystified but very much on the alert.

There was no need to tether Smoke, so Brant merely dropped the split bridle to the ground and left the big moro to his own devices, knowing that he would not stray. He assured himself that all the hands were sleeping on the upper bench, then walked to the edge of the cliff wall, settled himself in a comfortable position and waited.

Slowly the hours passed, and nothing happened. Brant's eyes grew heavy from constant staring into the dark. Despite the shelter afforded by the cliff overhang, his clothes became sodden with the rain mist that drifted in upon him. The sleeping cowboys, farther back, were better protected and the wind that chilled Brant to the bone did not reach them.

The silence persisted, broken only by the thin wail of the wind and the occasional impatient stamp of a horse. Brant heard the grunting and shifting as the cows stood up for the midnight "stretch," then the contented groaning and gurgling as they settled back to rest once more.

Another hour passed, with nothing happening, and then with the suddenness of a thunderclap the silence burst into horrific sound. Yells split the air, swung slickers snapped and crackled. There was a crashing of gunshots. Brant heard bullets thud into the blanket rolls laid in rows by the dying fire on the lower bench.

The cattle came to their feet with terrified bawls. Brant leaped forward a pace and both his guns streamed fire as he fired at the flashes on the prairie below. The exultant whoops of the raiders changed to yelps of alarm. The Running W hands came tumbling from their blankets, sized up the situation instantly and the boom of their guns added to the pandemonium. For moments the night was a blazing, roaring, bellowing hell. Then, with a low thunder of hoofs, the herd stampeded madly to the south. After them crashed the yelling raiders, lead whining through the darkness in their wake.

"After those cows! Round 'em up and start 'em millin'!" Brant shouted to the cursing cowboys. He turned to his own selected hands who were grouped close around him. "All right, fork your cayuses," he told them. "We'll give those wide-loopin' gents a mite of a surprise."

Around the cliff wall they bulged and up the long slope, speeding in the wake of Smoke who raced a length in the lead. They reached the crest of the rise, topped it and skalleyhooted down the far sag. For a mile Brant headed due north, then he veered to the west, his men swerving after him. Straight ahead the ominous loom of the hills showed dimly in the faint sheen of starlight that filtered through the cloud rack. As they drew nearer, a blacker segment made itself evident. It was the mouth of the canyon Brant had observed the evening before. He led his men into its gloom and halted.

"All right," he directed, "lead the horses over to one side and leave them in the brush. Those hellions should show any minute now. They'll have to circle back from the south with the bunch they cut out, but they won't be far behind us, or I'm making a big mistake. Get set. Let the cows go into the gulch. The sidewinders will be back to the rear, shoving them along. When they're close enough to line sights on, let 'em have it."

Tensely the cowboys waited, guns out and ready. For some minutes nothing happened. Then a low mutter shattered the silence. It grew to a rumble of many hoofs punctuated by the bleating of frightened steers. A dark mass came rolling across the prairie. Shouts sounded, and the sharper click of horses' irons. Jostling and clashing, the rustled cows poured into the blackness of the gorge. Behind loomed some six or seven horsemen.

"Let 'em have it!" roared Brant.

Instantly the cowboys' guns spouted fire. The canyon walls rocked to the thunder of the explosions. A terrified yell sounded. It was followed by the thud of a falling body, and another. There was a scream of pain, a gurgling cough, a wild clashing of bridle irons, then the frantic beat of hoofs fading into the distance. The Running W hands sent lead whining after the fleeing raiders until the uproar died away.

Brant lowered his smoking Colt. "We got a couple of 'em," he exulted. "I heard 'em hit the ground. Let's have a look-see. Careful, now, they're fangin' sidewinders and deadly as a back-busted rattler. Don't take a chance of leaning against a passing slug. Take it easy."

Cautiously, guns ready, the cowboys crept out of the shadows. On the ground at the mouth of the canyon lay what looked like two bundles of old clothes. Neither moved as the punchers approached. Brant took a chance and scratched a match. The tiny flare of light showed the two owl-hoots satisfactorily dead.

"This one is shot to pieces," he said, bending over the dead man. "The other's drilled plumb center, too. Say, this hellion looks familiar to me."

"Boss," exclaimed one of the hands, "it's that jigger you had the wring with back at the Dead-fall, the feller Phil Doran called Porter."

"Darned if it isn't," Brant agreed, scratching another match "And I'll bet a hatful of pesos he's the hellion I spotted riding herd on us all day yesterday over here in the brush. Well, he horned into one game too many!"

Dawn was breaking by the time the cowboys combed the wide-looped cows out of the canyon and started them back to the camp. When they got there, they found that the rest of the herd had been rounded up and was grazing quietly near the bed-ding ground. The night hawks had obeyed Brant's order and skalleyhooted at the first sign of danger. Nobody had been hurt, but Brant grimly surveyed the bullet holes in the bedrolls beside the rekin-dled fire.

"Snake-blooded bunch of hellions," he told Webb.

The old cowman removed his wide hat and mopped his face with a handkerchief.

"Gives me the creeps to think of what would have happened if we'd been bedded down here instead of on that upper bench," he said. "Son, you sure did a good chore and we all owe you a heap. How in blazes did you figger it out?"

"Yesterday," Brant explained, "I spotted a jigger over in the edge of the brush riding herd on us. He kept it up all day, and I had a hunch he wasn't doing all that riding just to exercise his horse. I figured he was there to find out just where we were going to bed down for the night and to get the lay of the land. Then he would hightail to a meeting place with the rest of his bunch and give them the lowdown. Chances were they were riding higher up in the hills, out of sight. When we did make camp, the thing was a perfect natural from their viewpoint. That canyon mouth is only about a mile distant from our camp. A plumb dark night. They could cut out a nice bunch of cows, slide them into that canyon and make an easy getaway. They figured we would be too busy rounding up the rest of the herd to trail after them, and even if we did, everything would be in their favor. So I decided the only thing to do was outsmart those gents. I gambled on their heading for the canyon with the bunch they cut out. Not that it was much of a gamble—the canyon was about the only place they could go. I also had a notion their sort wouldn't stop at a little thing like a cold-blooded killing or two. That's why I shifted the camp to the upper bench and left the bedrolls down on the lower bench as a come-on. They fell for it, all right."

"Outsmarted 'em is right!" growled Webb. "They're smartin' right now, I betcha, what's left of 'em. Figger you winged any more beside the two you downed?"

"There was some tall yelling when we cut down on them," Brant replied. "I've got a pretty good notion there was a punctured hide or two among the bunch that got away."

"Hope the hellions starve to death from leakin' their vittles out the holes," said Webb. "Well, mebbe we can make Dodge, now, without any more rukuses."

"Hope so," agreed Brant. "We should make it before dark, if things go right."

Chapter Four

Somebody once said, "The only difference between Dodge City and Hell is that you don't have to worry about anybody runnin' you outa Hell!"

Which wasn't much of an exaggeration when the Running W Trail herd rolled up to town.

The "Cowboy Capital" was at the height of its prosperity. When George Hoover and Jack McDonald pitched a tent on the site of the future cowtown, from which they sold whiskey to Fort Dodge soldiers, it is doubtful if they in the least envisioned what the future was to bring. Harry Lovett put up a second canvas saloon, and a gentleman with more elaborate notions, one Henry Sitler, built a sod house. This growing metropolis was called Buffalo City until the following spring brought railroad construction gangs. The railroaders mapped a town on the north side of the Arkansas River, five miles west of the fort. Very quickly, the ruts of the old Santa Fe Trail saw a general store and warehouse, three dancehalls and a half dozen saloons come into being. Dodge City was substituted for the really more descriptive "Buffalo City." Here at the end of steel—where the Santa Fe was pushing south to the Rio Grande—swiftly boomed a roaring, hell-raising, gun-smoking frontier town, the equal of which the nation was never to see again.

Smack up against the buffalo range, all Dodge City needed was railroad facilities to become the focal point of the hide business. And in those days buffalo hides were "Big Business." Thousands of hunters proceeded to collect millions of dollars for hides and meat and to spend the dinero in unequalled hell raisin'. Other throngs of wild and salty railroad builders added their payrolls to the flood of gold. Fully a thousand freight teams consisting of from eight to sixteen horses to a single great wagon hauled supplies south, west and north. The bull-whackers, mule-skinners and others attached to this industry were not of the modest violet type. Their chief ambition in life seemed to be to blow the wages of months in a single night of wild carousal in Dodge City. Several hundred soldiers and Indian scouts from Fort Dodge had similar notions. Dodge City was going strong, but hadn't really seen nothin' yet!

For the longhorns were on the march. The great herds began rolling up the Jones and Plummer Trail, and with them came their cowboy guardians with ideas of whoopin' it up that surpassed anything Dodge City had yet seen. Because of the element of competition involved, bull-whackers and mule skinners sort of didn't like railroaders and buffalo hunters. The sentiment was returned. Soldiers considered themselves better men than the gentlemen who drove mules, hunted buffalo or graded railroad, and were willing and ready to prove it at any time. Differences of opinion naturally arose, for the gentlemen who did not wear the blue couldn't see it that way. The result was gunsmoke in more than considerable quantities. The Texas cowboys had their own notions of who really belonged on top of the heap and backed it up with cartridges.

A proper seasoning for this kettle of "hell-broth" was provided by the gamblers, gunmen, owlhoots, "ladies" and others of similar ilk gathered from the four corners of the earth and run out of at least three and usually four.

All of which made Dodge City not exactly the place for a rest cure.

Of course, the Texans didn't like Northern men and were not slow in making the fact known. As they swaggered from saloon to gambling-hall to honky-tonk, jingling their spurs on high-heeled boots, their broad-brimmed "rainsheds" cocked jauntily over one eye, their six-guns much in evidence, they express their opinion in no uncertain tones. All of which somewhat irritated the older citizens. And not altogether without reason. The cowboys rode their horses on the sidewalks and into saloons. They took over the most attractive of the dance-hall girls. By way of variety they held up gambling games, and added insult to injury by throwing the dinero thus acquired across the bars, onto the green tables and into the ready hands of the "ladies." They shot the windows out of stores, proved their marksmanship by dusting the lights in various places with lead and by "dusting off" individuals who registered protest. It was all good fun, of course, but the humor was not always appreciated.

The most striking proof that all was not peaceful in Dodge was the fact that in Dodge's first season as a cow camp, twenty-five gentlemen were planted in Boot Hill, so called because the deceased were almost always buried with their boots, and other clothing, on. Lumber was too scarce and dear to waste on coffins.

At the time, Dodge was mostly Front Street, a wide road running east and west just north of the Santa Fe tracks. The principal cross street over the Arkansas River. For two blocks each way from Second Avenue, Front Street widened into what was known as the Plaza. The town's chief business establishments were strung along the north side of this square. Here were the Dodge House, Deacon Cox's famous hotel, Wright & Beverley's store, about the most important commercial establishment on the plains, the Delmonico Restaurant, the Long Branch Saloon, the Alamo Saloon, the City Drug Store, the Alhambra Saloon and the Dodge Opera House. The railroad depot, water tank and freight house were at the east end of the Plaza. Just south of the tracks was the calaboose or city jail, a one-roomed building constructed of two-by-six timbers. Perched on top of the flat roof was a flimsy structure the city judge and clerk used as an office.

South of the tracks were cheap hotels, honkeytonks, saloons without number, small-fry gambling houses and corrals.

To the north of Front Street, on a hill, was the residential section. An adjoining rise, the highest point in town, was occupied by what many considered the town's most thriving establishment—Boot Hill.

To the north of the railroad there was at least a semblance of law and order. South of the tracks, in Hell's Half Acres, between the railroad and the Arkansas River, most anything went, and most anything was the commonplace happening.

"I've seen Abilene, Wichita and Ellsworth, but this pueblo plumb passes the limit," old John remarked to Austin Brant. They had just finished a satisfactory conference with Webb's buyer and were walking slowly along Front Street in the early evening.

"You haven't seen anything yet, just wait till it gets dark," Brant prophesied. "By the way, I've a notion we ought to drop in and have a talk with the city marshal. His name is Tom Carney, I believe."

They found the marshal in his office. He was an affable man who greeted them pleasantly.

"I'd say the Dodge House is your best bet," he replied to the question Webb put to him. "It's usually quiet and orderly and Deacon Cox who runs it doesn't stand for any foolishness. Questionable characters aren't wanted there, and they know it. I certainly wouldn't advise you to go foolin' around south of the tracks. Everybody knows you run your big herd in today and that a buyer was here waiting for you to take over most of your cows. They'd be liable to figger the buyer paid off as soon as the cows were turned over to him.

"Besides, I don't expect much peace tonight. I got word that some of Dutch Harry's bunch are headed for town. They are out-and-out owlhoots and won't stop at anything. Soon as I hear where they land, I figger to drop a loop on them and corral them in the calaboose. Young hellions from the cow country raisin' cain is one thing, but jiggers with robbery and cold-blooded killin's in mind is somethin' else again. Under the circumstances, I'd stay indoors as much as possible while you're in town, if I was you."

"Good advice," agreed Webb. "Reckon I'm takin' it."

Before repairing to the hotel, Webb and Brant walked up the hill through the residential section. From its crest they could see a dozen herds held outside of town. The stockyards were crowded to the gates.

"Plenty of business, plenty of business," remarked the ranch owner. "And I figger the end ain't in sight yet."

Webb was right. An amazing market for Texas cows was developing with astounding rapidity. Four transcontinental lines of railroad were building. They made millions of acres of land accessible to home seekers. The push of the railroads into the Mississippi region made possible contact between the crowded population of the East and the rich grasslands of the West. Modern packing plants had already come into existence. Refrigerator cars were already running. Beef was being canned. To supply these markets and to stock the great ranges along the Rockies was up to the Texas longhorns. And at the moment, hell-roarin' Dodge was the focal point of distribution. Yes, there was "plenty of business," and more to come.

"I figure I'll look the town over a bit before hitting the hay," Brant told his Boss when they reached the hotel. "Like to see what makes it tick. And," he added, "I want to sort of keep an eye on the boys tonight. They'll be swallerforkin' all over the lot."

"Reckon they will," agreed Webb. "Go to it, son. Me, I'm takin' the marshal's advice and not sashayin' around with this hefty passel of money on me."

Dusk was falling when Brant left the hotel. He located a good restaurant and enjoyed a prime surroundin' of chuck. Then he sauntered out to look the town over.

"It was worth looking over, all right. With the advent of darkness, Dodge was really beginning to howl. Front Street was jammed with folks of all sorts moving to and fro on the board sidewalks, jostling, elbowing, laughing, swearing. In the street, riders were weaving in and out. Horses were tied to hitch racks, freight outfits were still unloading. The windows of saloons and gambling halls glowed as yellow as the gold that clinked the mahogany or slithered across the green cloth. The great mirror blazing bars were crowded, as were the tables and the other games. Mule-skinner, bull-whacker, cowboy, buffalo hunter and out-and-out badman rubbed shoulders. Orchestras blared, voices bellowed song, and boots thumped solidly on dance floors. The whir of roulette wheels vied with the sprightly clatter of flung dice. The chink of bottle neck on glass rim echoed the ring of the tossed gold piece. The afternoon rumble of Dodge was crescendoing to a star-quivering roar.

Brant dropped into the Long Branch saloon, run by Chalk Beeson and Bill Harris, and watched the famous Luke Short supervising the gambling. The Long Branch was noted for high stakes and the tenseness of the play induced more than ordinary quiet. After watching a poker game for a while where white chips were worth twenty dollars each, Brant decided on a look-see south of the railroad tracks.

Here the turbulence was at its height. Cowboys, whooping and yowling, raced their horses along the street, clattering onto the sidewalks at times, to the accompaniment of a wild scattering on the part of pedestrians. Somewhere sounded a stutter of shots, possibly only an outburst of exuberance, possibly something more serious. The saloons were not so well lighted as those on Front Street, but they were even more crowded. Gambling was not for so high stakes as in the Long Branch. As a recompense, it was accompanied by more noise, more arg'fyin' and more violence. The card sharps were just as adept, and deadlier than their compatriots of the Main Stem.

Stepping into a quieter saloon, Brant was rather surprised to encounter Norman Kane. The Flying V owner greeted him with his flashing smile and a pleasant nod.

"Boys are sort of whoopin' it up," he commented. "I came down to keep an eye on my hands. Reckon you're here for the same reason, eh?"

"Sort of," Brant admitted, "but I like to see the fun, too."

Kane made a wry face. "It's likely not to be so funny before the night is over," he predicted. "There are some hard characters down here. Plenty of snake blood. They're not all cowhands in for a bust."

Brant nodded soberly. "Let's have a drink," he suggested. Kane was agreeable and they moved to the bar. They were discussing the contents of their glasses when a young cowhand hurried in through the swinging doors, paused and glanced keenly about. With an exclamation of satisfaction, he strode up to Brant, who recognized one of his own riders.

"Boss," he said, "I was huntin' for you. Cooney said he saw you slide in here. There's a place down on Bridge Street, close to the river, where some of our boys are hangin' out. There's a bunch come in there and they aim to make trouble— clean out the place good. They're just waitin' for a couple more of their outfit to show up. The boys would like to get out, but figger if they try, trouble is liable to start." He glanced at Kane as he finished speaking. "You're the Flying V owner, ain't you, suh? There's a couple of your boys in there, too. And I heard," he added, "that the bunch is part of the Dutch Harry gang."

"Thanks for letting me know about it, Ray," Brant replied quietly. He turned to Kane. "Reckon we're both in this," he said. "First off, we'd better notify the marshal. He's on the lookout for the Harry bunch and will come along with us. That'll put the law on our side if anything busts loose."

"Good notion," applauded Kane. "Let's go."

Together they hurried to the marshal's office. They found Tom Carney in, and alone. He swore crisply when he heard what they had to say.

"I'll head down there pronto," he said. "My deputies are out somewhere, but I won't wait for 'em."

"We'll trail along, if it's agreeable with you," Brant said.

"Good!" exclaimed Carney. "I'll deputize you

both to help me in this business. I know the place your hand spoke about, Brant. All set? Here's a pair of handcuffs for each of you. Use 'em."

They hurried out. Carney led the way down Bridge Street almost to the river. "This is the place," he said, pausing before a poorly lighted saloon from which came the sound of loud voices raised in argument, a bellowing curse and the thud of a fall. "I'm scairt somethin's due to bust loose any minute. Kane, you stay outside and don't let anybody come up behind us. All set, Brant? Let's go!"

Shoulder to shoulder, the marshal and the Running W foreman pushed through the swinging doors. Outside, Norman Kane stood slender and erect with watchful eyes, and hands close to his gun butts.

Abruptly the turmoil inside the saloon hushed to a tense silence that endured for a crawling instant of suspense, then was shattered by the roar of gunfire. A moment later Marshal Carney reeled out, his body shot through and through, dying on his feet. Norman Kane sprang forward, caught the marshal's sagging body as he fell. He half carried, half dragged him beyond range of door and windows and eased him to the ground. Then he straightened up with a bitter curse and ran back. A gun in each hand, he plunged through the door, brought up short and stared in incredulous amazement.

Austin Brant, a smoking gun in one hand, was handcuffing two prisoners together, one wounded. In a circle around him lay three grotesquely sprawled forms. Directly in front of the menacing gun muzzle stood two men with their hands raised high.

Brant slanted a flickering glance sideways. "Put your cuffs on those two hellions," he directed Kane, gesturing slightly toward the hand-lifted pair with his gun muzzle. "Did they cash in the marshal?"

"I'm scairt they did," Kane replied as he manacled the scowling pair. "He looked like a dead man to me when I laid him on the sidewalk."

Brant bent his icy gaze on the prisoners for a moment, then he turned to where several cowboys, among them a glowering Cole Dawson, stood stiffly beside the bar. "Look after the marshal," he told them. "If he's still alive, get a doctor pronto. Come on, Kane, we'll herd these sidewinders to the calaboose. Get going, you, and don't stop, if you don't want to stop for good."

"Feller, why don't you take that big red-faced horned toad along, too?" one protested. "He started all this trouble—knocked Prouty down, busted his jaw."

Brant favored Cole Dawson with an ominous glance. "I'll take care of him later," he promised. "Get going, you two."

The prisoners sullenly obeyed. Brant and Kane marched them through the doors and onto the sidewalk, where a crowd had already gathered. There were mutterings and curses as they shoved their captives along, but nobody attempted to bar their progress.

Word of the shooting of the marshal had spread like wildfire. When Brant and Kane arrived at the calaboose with their charges, the city judge and a clerk were standing outside the door.

"Good work!" applauded the judge. "Take 'em upstairs."

They climbed the stairs and entered the office. The judge bent his gaze upon the prisoners. A gleam of recognition shone in his eyes.

"Say, don't you belong to Shang Pierce's outfit?" he asked one.

The prisoner nodded sullenly. "And this feller beside me does, too," he mumbled.

The judge and the clerk suddenly got their heads together. Brant and Kane heard fragments of muttered sentences—Biggest shipper out of Texas—Bad for business—Might go elsewhere."

The judge turned to Brant. "Was it either of these fellers plugged the marshal?" he asked.

"No," replied Brant. "These fellers didn't get going. The ones who plugged the marshal are still down Bridge Street, on the floor. I figure they'll stay there until somebody packs them away."

The judge nodded, tugged his goatee. "Then I reckon," he said, "these fellers ain't guilty of anything but disturbin' the peace. I'll fine 'em twenty-five dollars each and turn 'em loose. Give them their guns back, Mr. Clerk."

Grinning, the prisoners paid their fine. The judge waved them out.

"Just a minute," Brant said as they turned to go. His eyes were the color of windswept ice as they rested on the quartette. "The only reason you didn't pull on the marshal was because I had your owlhoot friends on the floor and the drop on you before you could clear leather. I just want that straight for the record. Don't belt those guns on in here. Now get going, and don't look back. Turn the next corner, and turn it fast!"

Brant followed them to the door. The four obeyed orders to the letter. Then Brant re-entered the room.

"Come on, Kane," he said, "let's get out of here."

"Wait," called the clerk, an unctious, pompous little man. "Judge," he said, "this young feller did a good chore just the same. I got a notion we could do worse than appoint him town marshal in place of Carney. What say, young feller, want the job? Two hundred dollars a month is the pay."

Austin Brant looked him up and down. "Dodge City, it seems," he said, "figures marshals at twenty-five dollars a head. I figure I'm worth a mite more."

He turned his back on the two officials and walked to the door. As he stepped out, a hand touched his elbow. He turned to face a tall blond man with a drooping mustache and the keenest and coldest blue eyes Brant had ever seen.

"Feller," said the tall man, his deep rumbling voice reminding Brant of a lion's growl, "you did a first rate chore, and you made a first rate answer. Congratulations! You're a man to ride the river with!"

"Much obliged," Brant nodded and passed on, Kane strolling elegantly behind him. Brant was pleased with the compliment. He would have been more pleased had he known that the man who paid it was the man who would later clean up Dodge City and make it safe for decent folks, just as he cleaned up Ellsworth and Wichita, the greatest peace officer the West ever knew—Wyatt Berry Stapp Earp!

Chapter Five

Outside the building, Brant and Kane paused. "Well," said the latter, "after all the excitement, I feel I can do with another drink. But not down here. Let's go up to Front Street, where we can down our likker without havin' to stand back to back."

Brant agreed and they crossed the tracks and entered the Alamo Saloon. When they pushed through the swinging doors, conversation in the big room abruptly ceased. Eyes slanted and heads wagged in their direction.

"Didn't take long for the news to get around," Kane muttered. "Feller, you're a marked man in this town."

"Not much to brag about," Brant grunted disgustedly. "Reckon the only way to get noticed is to plug somebody. Not that there's anything particularly outstanding about that. I've a notion there's hardly a hellion in this pueblo who hasn't shot somebody at one time or another."

"But they didn't down three of Dutch Harry's bunch at one settin'," Kane replied. "Well, here's how!"

As Brant and Kane quietly discussed their drinks, conversation gradually resumed. By the time they left the saloon, it was in full uproar again. They decided to call it a night and headed for the Dodge House. They found John Webb seated in the lobby with several oldtimers. Webb bent a searching gaze on Brant, nodded cordially to Kane.

"Come here, Austin," he called to his foreman. "Want you to get to know Shanghai Pierce. Reckon you've heard of him."

Brant had, along with most everybody else in the cow country.

Abel Pierce, better known as Shanghai or Shang Pierce, was the most unusual and the most striking in appearance of all the cattle barons of the West. He was not a Texan, but a transplanted Connecticut Yankee. Long association with the Southwest, however, had stamped him with its characteristics. When he went about buying cattle, he rode a splendid black horse rigged out with all the accouterments dear to the cowhand. He was accompanied by a Negro servant who led a pack-horse loaded with gold and silver. He would empty the money on a blanket and pay it out to the stockmen when the cows were delivered. His cows became known from the Rio Grande to the Canadian Line as Shanghai Pierce's sea-lions.

The things he did were startling, sometimes outrageous, often mirth-provoking. For instance, when Nebraska was busted, he offered the local government a ten thousand dollar annual payment for the exclusive privilege of dealing monte on railroad trains within the state's borders. The legislators didn't know just how to take it, and while they were debating the question, Shanghai amended his proposition and offered the same money for the right to deal the game against only such passengers as professed to be clergymen or missionaries. The Frontier roared, but the legislators couldn't see the humor of the situation and turned Shanghai down. Whereupon Shanghai, bound to spend his ten thousand dollars some way, got rid of it by setting up a bronze statue, forty feet high, of himself in cowboy rig on his Rancho Grande headquarters at Tres Palacios.

This was only one of many of Shang Pierce's humorous doings, but his drives were the largest to hit the Chisholm Trail, and other owners had a habit of following where Shang went. Which made him rather more than welcome at any shipping town.

Pierce was six feet four in height and weighed two hundred and twenty pounds. He had a full beard and snapping eyes. When he stood up to shake hands with Austin Brant, those eyes were about on a level with Brant's.

"Heard about you, son, heard about you," he boomed. "Heard you did a good chore down on Bridge Street. Hauled in a couple of my young hellions too, eh? Wait till I clap eyes on 'em. They'll hear from me proper—mixin' up with the Dutch Harry bunch. Didn't either one of 'em do any of the shootin', though, did they?"

"No," Brant replied, a trifle grimly, "they didn't."

Pierce didn't miss what Brant's tone of voice implied. His answer sounded enigmatical, but Brant also understood. "Uh-huh," Pierce nodded, "men who work for me usually are sort of lucky."

His voice abruptly became serious—and kindly.

"But take an old man's advice, son. Watch your *step*. From now on you're a marked man. The Dutch Harry bunch is bad. They'll be out to even up the score. To even it up with you and that big feller who is with your outfit, what's his name—Dawson? They blame Dawson for starting all the trouble, and blame you for finishing it. They won't forget, and they won't let up. In fact, it would be better if you were both out of this hell town. Something's got to be done about it. I talked with the mayor and the city judge a little while ago. We've taken one step to help. We got Billy Brooks to take the job of chief marshal, and he's picked a couple of salty deputies. Brooks has a long list of killings to his credit, all in fair fight. I've a notion he'll do something toward cleaning up the pueblo.

"We tried to get Wyatt Earp to take the job, after you turned it down, but he just laughed and said, 'That young feller Brant gave my answer before I got a chance to say it. Maybe later, after they elect some town officials with guts, I may take the chore. But not now, Shang, not now. I got other things to do.' Understand he's headin' south. Well, goodnight, Webb, don't forget the things I told you. And goodnight, son. Don't forget what I just told you, either."

The jovial cattle baron and his cronies took their departure and stamped off to bed. Webb immediately requested a first-hand account of the happenings in the Bridge Street saloon. He shook his head when Brant finished.

"I don't like it, son," he said. "I don't like it. I've been hearin' things about Dutch Harry and his bunch. There's about twenty more of 'em maverickin' around this section, and they won't ever forgive you for downin' three of their sidewinders. They'll be out to get you. What happened tonight made up my mind for me on somethin' I been figgerin' about. This town ain't no place for you right now, and the quicker you get out the better. I figger to hang around a spell, until I dispose of the rest of the cows. Shang Pierce lined me up on somethin'. There's a buyer headed this way from Deadwood. They need meat bad at that gold camp and will pay almighty high prices for it. Old Shang sort of took a shine to me, I reckon, for he offered to tie me up with that buyer. It's too good a chance to miss. He'll be here some time tomorrow. Also I aim to sell the remuda. Can get a fancy price for them cayuses. It may take a little time, but I figure it'll pay me to stick around till I do it."

Brant nodded. Webb was silent for a moment, apparently turning something over in his mind.

"So you see I can't very well pull up stakes right away," he added. "But Wes Morley of the Bar M has a banknote to meet and I promised him the money to pay it off as soon as I got back from this drive. The way things are shapin' up, it looks like I won't get back in time to do him any good. So I figure to send you home with the dinero I got for the cows I sold today and what I'll get from the Deadwood buyer tomorrow. Figure you can start day after tomorrow. Wish I was goin' with you. Wish we were all gettin' out of this hell town pronto. I'm scairt somebody will get into trouble."

Webb's fears were well grounded. Somebody did get into trouble, very serious trouble, and as might have been expected, it was blundering, belligerent Cole Dawson. The Dutch Harry crowd didn't forget.

Chapter Six

The whole senseless business started over practically nothing. There was a poker game in the Half Acre saloon, south of the tracks. Cole Dawson was losing, and he didn't like it. Cole could hardly be called a good loser.

Poker is a funny game. A man who can't win himself, may even be losing, is like as not walloping the socks off another unfortunate, and passing his winnings on to others. One of the players was a storekeeper, a quiet, inoffensive man named Cullen Brady. He wasn't winning. In fact, he was losing a bit. But every time he tangled with Cole Dawson in a pot, Dawson dropped his eye teeth. The fact that Brady immediately lost what he raked in to somebody else didn't soothe Dawson's feelings. Brady was the player primarily responsible for Dawson being way behind the game. His wrath focused on the inoffensive storekeeper. He rumbled, growled and favored Brady with venomous glances. Brady said nothing and went on playing his game.

Brady shuffled cards expertly. His slim-fingered hands were a poem of movement as he flipped the pasteboards to the table. He had just dealt when Dawson lost a particularly large pot he had been sure of winning, to Brady. His face turned even redder with anger. He glowered across the table at the storekeeper.

"Feller," he said, "you're mighty handy with cards. That last riffle looked to me like a tinhorn riffle."

There was a murmur of protest. Everybody present knew Brady played an absolutely square game.

The storekeeper looked at Dawson. He was no coward. He said flatly:

"You lie!"

Dawson's face turned crimson, his eyes blazed. He reached across the table and slapped Brady across the mouth, hard, knocking him from his chair. Again there arose an angry protest, louder this time.

Brady got to his feet, wiped the blood from his lips and looked at Dawson.

"I'm no match for you, and I'm not a gunfighter," he said quietly. "I guess I'll have to take it."

He cashed in his chips and left the saloon, leaving a decidedly strained atmosphere behind.

Three men standing together at the bar saw it all. They had been watching the game with interest. One, a lean, lanky individual with a crooked scar welting his cheek, turned to the others and said something in a low voice. The three heads drew together for a moment, then the scar-faced man nodded and strolled out.

Dawson did not stay in the game much longer. The attitude of the other players was decidedly chilly. He cashed what few chips he still held, slouched to the bar and ordered a drink. He was glowering at his empty glass when a man walked in, glanced about and approached Dawson. He tapped him on the shoulder. Dawson turned an angry face in his direction.

"Dawson, you don't know me, and I don't know you, either, except by name," the man said in low tones. "But I know your Boss, old man Webb, real well. I like him and wouldn't want something bad to happen to one of his hands."

"What the hell you talkin' about?" Dawson growled.

"I'm just giving you a little friendly advice," said the other. "When you leave here, turn right, go down the street and around the corner. Don't go up the street. Cullen Brady and two of his friends are standing in front of the Montezuma Bar, right up the street. I reckon they're waiting for you to show."

Dawson grew still angrier. He spat an oath. "Feller," he rumbled, "do you figure I'm goin' to put my tail between my legs and trail my twine because of any blankety-blank that walks with the forked end down?"

"It's not a case of puttin' your tail between your legs, as I see it," said the other. "It's just a case of draw or drag, and you Texas fellers ain't fast and accurate enough for these northern gun slingers."

That did it. Cole Dawson had plenty of faults, but lack of courage was certainly not one of them. And the slur at a Texan's gun handling ability touched him on the raw. He glared at the speaker, turned and pounded out of the saloon. When he got outside, he didn't turn down the street. He turned up it, still growling profanity.

Before he had walked half a block, Dawson spotted Cullen Brady. He was standing in front of the

Montezuma, all right, the light streaming through the windows gleaming on his white shirt. With him were two other men.

Hand on his gun butt, Dawson kept right on going. He was perhaps ten paces from Brady when a shot rang out. Not from where Brady stood but from the shadows beneath a shuttered building across the street. Dawson felt the wind of the passing bullet. With a bellow of rage he jerked his gun and fired two shots at the flash.

The gun from the shadows blazed again. Other shots sounded on Dawson's side of the street. He jerked his head around.

Cullen Brady was lying where he had stood a moment before, prone on his face. A widening blotch dyed the back of his white shirt crimson. The two men who had been talking to him had taken to their heels and were vanishing around the corner.

Sputtering bewildered curses, Dawson lumbered forward and bent over Brady, staring at his bloody back. He heard purposeful steps behind him, but was so flabbergasted by it all he didn't turn his head.

Something hard and cold jammed against his ribs. "Drop that iron!" said a voice.

Dawson screwed his head around and stared into the ice-blue eyes of Marshall Billy Brooks.

"Drop it!" Brooks repeated. "And straighten up." The click of his gun hammer emphasized the command.

Cole Dawson did not know Brooks personally, but he knew him by sight and knew of his reputation. He let his gun fall to the ground and straightened up.

"What's the big notion?" he demanded angrily.

"Shut up!" Brooks told him. "I'll do the talking. This way, boys," he called, raising his voice.

Two or more men came hurrying up. They were Jack Allen and Henry Brown, Brooks' newly-appointed deputies, and just as salty as the marshal himself.

"Give Brady a once-over," Brooks ordered. "See if he's heeled."

"He isn't packing any hardware," Allen announced a moment later.

"He never did," put in Brown. "Everybody knows that."

"And shot in the back," Brooks remarked grimly. "Take this sidewinder and lock him up."

A deputy on either side, Dawson, still cursing and protesting, was led away. Brooks picked up Dawson's gun and pocketed it.

"Some of you fellers rig up a stretcher or get a shutter and we'll take Brady to the coroner's office," he told the gathering crowd.

Word of what had happened got around swiftly, and the town boiled. Killings were one thing, but shooting an unarmed man in the back was too much for even Dodge to stomach. It was a foregone conclusion that when the coroner's jury brought in its verdict, an example would be made of Cole Dawson.

"Well, I always said that loco jughead would end up stretching rope," old John Webb observed resignedly. "Guess there's nothing we can do about it. Like asking for a necktie party yourself to side with Dawson."

Austin Brant's black brows drew together in a perplexed frown.

"Boss," he said, "there's something mighty

funny about this business. To my mind it just doesn't make sense. There's plenty wrong with Cole Dawson, granted, but Cole Dawson wouldn't shoot an unarmed man in the back, nor an armed one, for that matter. He just isn't made that way."

"Maybe not," grunted Webb, "but Cullen Brady sure got shot in the back. There's a hole in his back and none in his front."

Brant's eyes grew thoughtful. "Which means the bullet is still in his body."

"Sounds reasonable," Webb admitted. "Of course it might have been an accident, somehow."

"A mighty convenient accident, seems to me," Brant replied grimly. "And the bullet's still in him. Let's go down and see Dawson."

At the jail they were admitted to Dawson's presence. They found Cole surly and defiant. Brant didn't waste time consoling him.

"Dawson," he said, "you and me don't always see things eye to eye, but we'll pass that up. I want you to tell me, did you shoot Brady?"

"Shoot him, hell!" Dawson exploded. "I didn't even shoot in his direction. I shot two shots at somebody who was throwin' lead at me from out of the dark across the street."

"You didn't see anybody over there?"

"No! I told you it was dark. I just saw the gun flashes."

"They could have been holed up behind something, then."

"Could have been. I sure didn't see 'em."

"Did you see anybody else shooting?"

"I didn't see anybody, but I sure heard somebody," Dawson replied. "Somebody up the street. That's when I looked around and saw two fellers runnin' around the corner, and Brady layin' on his face. I tried to tell the marshal that, but he just laughed at me. Reckon the jury'll do the same."

"Most likely," Brant agreed. "It does sound sort of loco. Now tell me one more thing. Were you packing your own gun last night?"

"I don't ever pack no other," Dawson growled.

"And the marshal has it?"

"Reckon he has, he picked it up and stuck it in his pocket," Dawson answered. "Why?"

"Nothing much, but if I get the break I'm hoping for, you can thank your lucky stars that there are mighty few Smiths, especially the Russian Model, around in this section. Come on, John, I want to see the coroner."

They left behind a profane and bewildered Dawson.

The coroner turned out to be a white-whiskered old frontier doctor with a truculent eye. Brant introduced Webb and himself.

"Doctor," Brant asked, "where is the bullet that killed Cullen Brady?"

"Inside him," replied the doctor, jerking his head toward a sheeted form in the back room.

"I'd like for you to dig it out."

The old doctor bristled. "What's the sense in that?" he demanded. "There ain't no need for an autopsy in this case. No doubt as to the cause of Brady's death."

"So I gather," Brant nodded. "You're certain, then, that Brady's death was caused by the bullet now lodged in his body?"

"Of course I'm certain," answered the doctor. "Why do you want me to remove that slug?"

"Because," Brant said quietly, "by doing so you may save an innocent man from being hanged."

The coroner stared, started to argue, then apparently changed his mind.

"Okay," he said, "I'll do it."

He got out his instruments and went to work, while Brant and Webb sat in the outer office and smoked. In a short time the doctor came out, wiping something with a cloth. He held forth a bid of lead.

"Here it is," he said. "Not battered much, either. Went through the soft tissue of the heart and ended up in the big muscle that runs alongside the spine."

Brant took the slug and turned it over in his fingers, his keen eyes narrowing as they concentrated on the object. He looked up to meet the coroner's expectant gaze.

"Not hard to see, even with the naked eye," he remarked. "But I suppose you've got a magnifying glass handy? Put the glass on it. I guess you know considerable about guns. Remember Dawson was packing a Smith & Wesson."

The doctor procured his glass and peered through it at the bullet.

"See them?" Brant asked, revolving his finger in a spiral motion.

"By gosh son, you're right!" exploded the coroner. "How in hell did you come to think of it?"

"It just sort of came to me," Brant deprecated. "You see, what happened didn't fit into the picture with Cole Dawson, that's all. He's ornery as hell in some ways, but he didn't size up to this sort of thing."

"Well, he can thank the Good Lord that some-body felt that way about him," said the coroner. "You'll be at the inquest, of course—two hours from now?"

"I will," Brant promised. "Bring the slug along. And have Marshal Brooks bring Dawson's gun. Keep quiet about this, Boss," he cautioned Webb.

As the inquest got under way, things looked bad for Cole Dawson, and as it progressed they looked blacker. To all appearances it was an open-and-shut case. Marshal Brooks told how he found Dawson standing over Brady's body, the smoking gun in his hand. The poker game row was cited in detail, as a motive for the killing. Impartial ob-servers agreed that Dawson had been violently angry with Brady; that later he had stalked out of the saloon, his face working with rage, his hand on the butt of his gun. The shooting in the street was heard a few moments later. Nobody came forward who had seen the actual killing. It was plain the jury considered Dawson's story fantas-tic. The faces of the jurymen were set like stone when Austin Brant arose and requested leave to address the jury. Doc McChesney, the coroner, readily granted the request. His expression be-trayed a trace of sardonic amusement.

"Gentlemen," Brant began informally, "I've a notion I'm safe in assuming that you all know considerable about guns." He paused, expectant. There was a general nodding of heads.

"So," Brant continued, "I'd like to ask you a question. How are Colt revolvers rifled?"

The jury looked surprised, then the foreman spoke up.

"They're rifled with a left-hand twist and six grooves." The others nodded agreement.

"And how about Smith & Wesson revolvers?" Brant asked.

There was a stir of excitement in the crowded courtroom. Some folks were beginning to get the drift.

"How about Smith & Wesson?" Brant repeated. Again the foreman spoke up.

"A Smith is rifled with a right-hand twist and five grooves."

"All except one model, the Texan," Brant corrected. He turned to the crowd, raising his voice.

"Anybody want to argue with what's been said?" he asked.

There was a general shaking of heads.

"Okay," said Brant. "And I guess everybody will admit that it's easy to spot the riflings on a bullet that's been fired, if it isn't badly smashed up."

Again there were only nods of agreement.

Brant turned to the coroner. "Doctor McChesney," he said, "will you please produce the bullet that killed Cullen Brady, the bullet you removed from his body in the presence of myself and John Webb? Thank you. Please hand it to the jury foreman, and to make it easier for him, let him use your magnifying glass."

The foreman accepted the bullet and the glass. The others crowded around him.

"Well?" Brant asked as the foreman looked up.

"Well," said the foreman, "this slug waren't never fired from a Smith & Wesson six, that's for certain. "Looks to be a .44, but she came out of a Colt. The riflings show that, plain."

"Exactly," said Brant. "Now will Marshal

Brooks please produce the gun he took off Cole Dawson, the gun Dawson was holding as he bent over Cullen Brady's body? Thank you, Marshal. Please pass it to the jury."

Cole Dawson's old Smith & Wesson was passed from hand to hand, to an accompaniment of mutters and wagging heads. The foreman turned to the coroner.

"Well, Doc, it looks like we came damn near to hangin' the wrong man," he said. "The Dawson feller never shot Brady with this hogleg. Guess he never shot Brady at all, 'less he had another gun and swallered it, which don't sound reasonable."

The jury didn't even take the trouble to retire to consider a verdict. They sat around and smoked while the foreman laboriously wrote it out. When he finished, it read—

Cullen Brady came to his death at the hands of a party or parties unknown. We recommend that the marshal find out and run down the hellions as quickly as possible.

There followed a typical cow country rider—

And we further recommend that the town try to hire that smart young fellow, Austin Brant, to help him do it.

Cole Dawson was released at once. He evinced very little relief, only glowered at Austin Brant.

"Feller," he said, "guess the right thing for me to do is say much obliged. Reckon I'll have to. But

I'm gettin' deeper and deeper in your debt all the time, and I don't like it."

Old John Webb opened his mouth to speak his mind, then closed it again with nothing said. What the hell was the use!

But that night in the hotel lobby, with Norman Kane sitting beside them, he spoke very earnestly to Austin Brant.

"Remember what I told you?" he said. "That Dutch Harry bunch is snake-blooded and smart. They deliberately set out to frame poor Dawson for a hanging, and if it hadn't been for you, they'd have gotten away with it. And they'll hold that against you, too. Well, when they come looking for you, you won't be here. I've got to get that money to Wes Morley in time for him to meet his bank note. So you're headin' south with the dinero, and it's a hefty passel come early mornin'."

Brant had his doubts about Wes Morley's urgent need of money, but he couldn't very well argue with the Boss. He could see that Webb was anxious to get him away from Dodge City as quickly as possible. The Morley matter made a good excuse.

"I got my powders," he replied. "Be ready to ride come daylight."

"Good!" Webb nodded. He turned to Norman Kane. "Those hellions won't forget you had a hand in the business, too, Kane," he remarked. "Better watch your step."

"Don't figger to be here long anyhow," Kane returned easily. "Got important business to attend to in Oklahoma. Well, I'm headed for bed. *Buenos Noches.*"

"Feller uses a heap of Spanish for an Okie," Webb remarked as Kane left the lobby.

"Don't rec'lect him saying he was from Oklahoma—just said he owned a spread there," Brant pointed out.

"That's right, he could be from down along the border," Webb agreed.

Brant was up by daylight to prepare for his long ride back to the Texas Panhandle. Before leaving the hotel, he thought of saying goodbye to Norman Kane, if the latter was out of bed. He stopped at the desk to inquire.

"Mr. Kane checked out shortly after midnight," he clerk replied, after consulting the register.

"Checked out! Didn't say where he was going?"

"Evidently not," the clerk replied. "There is no notation."

Brant nodded and left the hotel. "Decided to stick closer to his men, after the rukus last night, chances are," he reasoned.

Shortly afterward, Smoke's irons were clicking on the boards of the toll bridge. With no bad luck, Brant hoped to cover the nearly seventy miles to Doran's Crossing by dark. He knew Smoke was good for the distance, travelling at a fast pace. The trail was not bad and few difficulties of terrain offered between Dodge City and the Cimarron. He would spend the night at the Crossing, ford the river the following morning and then cover the three hundred odd miles to the Running W at a more leisurely pace. But with the thousands Webb had received for the cows carefully tucked away in inside pockets, he desired to put distance between him and the Cowboy Capital as quickly as possible. Somebody might very well have guessed the reason for his abrupt departure from Dodge. He was not particularly uneasy, however, for it was not likely that any gentlemen with "notions" would have figured he intended riding from Dodge this morning.

Barely had he crossed the bridge when Brant saw the first dust cloud rolling up from the south. A few minutes later he was flashing past the first great herd headed for Dodge City. Soon there was another dust cloud and another herd. Then another, and another, till it seemed to the Running W foreman that the endless miles between Kansas and the plains of Texas were one vast sea of rolling eyes, shaggy backs and clashing horns.

"Wouldn't seem there were that many critters on all the Southwest rangeland," he mused as he waved reply to the riders shoving along their reluctant charges.

All day long he passed the herds, some large, some small, but all rolling northward toward the waiting markets. The longhorns were on the march!

Brant's saddlebags were crammed with provisions. Around midday he paused beside a spring and cooked a comforting surroundin' to which he did ample justice. Smoke grazed contentedly the while, apparently none the worse for the many miles he had galloped. After eating Brant rode on. The stars were shining brightly when he at last sighted the lights of Doran's Crossing.

"A little helpin' of chuck and a drink, and then I hope I can get a decent bunk to sleep on in that shebang," he told Smoke. "I'll just rack you outside till I get the lowdown on what's what. Ought not to be any trouble tieing onto a nosebag for you."

Tethering the moros at a convenient hitchrack, he entered the Deadfall. The big room was less crowded than on his former visits, and quieter. He recognized several Texans with whom he had a passing acquaintance and nodded to them. Standing at the far end of the bar, per usual, were massive, black-bearded Phil Doran and his wizened, ice-eyed partner, Pink Hanson. Brant nodded to them, and they nodded back. He saw the partners' heads draw together. As they talked, they shot glances in his direction.

Brant was discussing his drink when Doran left the end of the bar and came sauntering in his direction. The Deadfall owner paused, and looked Brant up and down.

"See you met up with poor Cort Porter out on the prairie, Brant," he remarked casually.

Brant stared at Doran in astonishment. Under the circumstances of his meeting with Porter, it was the last thing he would have expected of Doran, to admit knowledge of Porter's activities north of the Cimarron.

"Yes, I met up with him," he replied.

"Uh-huh, so I figgered," Doran said. "Wasn't a very nice thing to do, Brant, even if you did have a run-in with him here—to shoot a poor jigger in the back."

Brant stared again. His eyes narrowed slightly. He did not at the moment reply to Doran's astounding charge.

"Uh-huh," Doran repeated, "not a very nice thing to do. The boys found him, or what was left of him, out there by the canyon mouth."

Brant spoke. "If the boys, whoever they were,

found him, they know damn well he wasn't shot in the back, and they know, too, how he come to get shot," he replied quietly, his gaze hard on Doran's florid face.

"Porter was my bunky," Doran went on, as if not even hearing Brant's statement. "And I'm tellin' you, Brant, I'm out to even up the score for him."

Instinctively, Brant's thumbs hooked over his cartridge belts. The significance of the gesture was not lost on Doran. He shook his bristling head.

"Nope, not that way," he said. "I know I wouldn't have any more chance with you at gun slingin' than a rabbit would have in a houndawg's mouth. I know you're a quick-draw man, and I know that's what you rely on to get you by. Feller always uses an ace-in-the-hole to back up a yaller streak. But if you weren't packin' them irons, I'd put a head on you you wouldn't forget for a spell, you low-down hyderphobia skunk!"

Brant's face went a little white. He was boiling with anger but he kept a grip on himself.

"I figger you must have been drinking your own snake juice, Doran," he said. "Either that or you've gone plumb loco, but I reckon in either case I'll have to ram your words down your throat."

He turned, glanced about. Swiftly unbuckling his belts he handed them to a big Texas cowboy he knew slightly.

"Hold 'em," he said. "Have 'em ready for me if I should happen to need 'em," he added significantly.

The Texan took the belts. "I'll hold 'em," he promised, adding with grim emphasis, "and I'll use 'em, too, if necessary." He swept the gathering crowd with hard eyes. "No interferin', gents,' he warned, "or things will get lively."

Brant faced the bulky Deadfall owner. "Okay, Doran, you're called," he said. He cast a quick glance toward Pink Hanson, who was standing back of Doran and a little to one side. In Hanson's pale eyes was a peculiar look of malicious satisfaction, the look of one whose well-thought-out plans are coming to fruition. It puzzled Brant, but before he could give it much consideration, he had another matter to think about.

Austin Brant was a fighter and he could hit like the kick of a mule, but like the average cowhand, the science of boxing was a closed book to him. Phil Doran, on the other hand, had somewhere in the course of his dubious career, picked up more than a little knowledge of the art of self-defense. He was quick as a cat on his feet, despite his bulk, and he knew how to use his hands.

As Brant charged in, he was met by a vicious jab to the mouth that brought blood and staggered him. Before he could recover, Doran hit him again, left and right, with plenty of power behind the blows. Brant reeled, almost lost his footing. Doran glided in. But Brant was far from out. He ducked a left hook, countering with a swinging right that knocked Doran sideways against the bar. With plenty of courage, but little judgment, Brant rushed. Doran slipped away, feinted with his left, brought over a straight right and knocked Brant off his feet.

The Texas cowboy bounded erect almost before

he hit the floor and bored in, swinging with both hands. A cool and experienced Doran, ducked, weaved and covered up, getting in several hard jabs at the same time. Again Brant was forced to give ground. And Doran was after him, jabbing, hooking, drawing blood, staggering the tall cowhand with lethal rights and lefts. Brant was breathing hard, his face was cut and bloody, his eyes already swelling. As he lurched back a little farther, he glimpsed Pink Hanson's face once more. It was ablaze with exultation. His eyes glowed.

And in that fleeting glance, a blinding light of understanding struck Brant. With hair-trigger suddenness he realized the trap that had been set for him, into which he had so blithely walked. The explanation for Doran's astounding championing of the dead rustler, Porter. Brant knew very well that Phil Doran had no more loyalty to anybody than a coyote. He saw now that he had been goaded into a wring he was bound to lose. Somehow, Doran had found out, or had divined that he, Brant, was packing the money John Webb received for his herd. Doran was out to get that money, and he had a mighty good chance to get it, too.

As a fist fighter, Brant knew he was out-classed by the Deadfall owner. In a few minutes, he would be knocked cold. Then Doran and his snake-blooded partner, with "chivalrous solicitude" for Doran's defeated adversary, would pack him off to one of the Deadfall bedrooms until he had recovered from his beating. Doubtless a tap on the head with a gun barrel would insure that the recovery not to be too speedy. And when Brant would finally wake up, the money he carried would be gone. And not a thing to prove that Doran had anything to do with its disappearance.

All this passed through Brant's mind in a flash while he ducked and parried and tried to get away from Doran's shower of blows. He saw Doran's eyes glitter with triumph as he maneuvered for the kill. He took a last chance, a desperate gamble that might succeed. As Doran feinted with his left to bring Brant's guard down, his right in position for the knock-out blow, Brant hurled himself downward at Doran's knees. The impact knocked the big man off his feet. As he sprawled on the floor, Brant surged erect, gripping Doran's flailing ankles in both hands. With all his strength, he plucked the Deadfall owner from the floor and whirled him around and around. At the apex of the swing he altered its directions and brought Doran crashing down upon the floor. Doran gave a gasping groan, stiffened out and lay motionless, face white, arms wideflung.

Brant whirled, plucked his gun belts from the astounded Texas cowboy and slid one of the long Colts from its sheath. He faced Pink Hanson and the tense group behind him. Hanson, his mouth slightly ajar with astonishment at the sudden and unexpected end to the wring, stared back. Their glances crossed, perfect understanding in each. Hanson's face twisted with baffled fury. Then the look of rage was supplanted by one of grudging admiration. Pink Hanson looked the six feet and more of Austin Brant up and down with the respect of one fighting man for another. His mouth snapped shut to its normal rat-trap tightness. He nodded, the nod of a loser who knows he has lost.

"By God!" he said. "Feller, you're a man!"

Brant nodded reply. He was in no shape for speech. Awkwardly, still holding his drawn Colt on Hanson and his companions, he buckled his belts in place. Then he backed warily to the door, fighting a deadly nausea that threatened to crumple him up. The Texans present, not in the least understanding what it was all about, muttered their astonishment. Still watchful, Brant vanished between the swinging doors. He staggered to his horse, and with his last strength crawled into the saddle. He turned Smoke's head toward the river. He knew he must put distance between himself and the Deadfall before Doran recovered.

"We won't eat tonight, feller," he muttered as he surged Smoke into the water. A moment later they were both swimming. To Brant's ears came the faint sound of shouts.

The cold water revived Brant somewhat, so that he was able to mount again when they reached the shallows near the south bank. Swinging forward on the horse's neck, he twined his fingers in Smoke's coarse mane and held on, giving the moros his head. Another moment and the big blue horse was speeding southward at a fast clip.

Brant rode for many miles. Finally he pushed the moros into the heart of a dense thicket, tumbled to the ground and almost instantly was asleep.

Chapter Seven

Sunshine was streaming down and birds were singing in the bushes when Brant finally awoke. He was stiff and sore all over; his eyes were nearly closed and his face was like a piece of raw beefsteak, but he felt greatly refreshed. With the elasticity of youth, he had thrown off the effects of the bad beating, the exhausting swim and the miles of hard riding. As he got a fire going and coffee on the boil, he was whistling as merrily through his cut lips as were the birds on the branches.

"Reckon that sidewinder knows he was in a wrong, too," he chuckled. "Bet I loosened every joint in his ornery carcass when I slammed him on the floor."

The feel of the packets of money was as comforting as the food he consumed with ravenous appetite. Then he dried out his tobacco in the sun and enjoyed a refreshing smoke.

"Let's go, feller," he told the grazing horse. "We got a long ride ahead of us still, but I've a notion we won't meet up with any more trouble. Whoever managed to get word to Doran and his hellions that we were packing all this dinero hardly had time to get ahead of us again. We'll make Texas okay. I'll be glad to see the old Palo

Duro again. To heck with this Kansas and Oklahoma country! Folks don't act nice up here."

As he rode away from the thicket, Brant puzzled greatly as to how Doran could have known he carried Webb's money. He was sure that the Deadfall owner would never have taken such a chance based on mere guesswork.

"Nope, somebody must have hightailed mighty fast to get to the Crossing before I did. The question is, who? I can't for the life of me figure who knew what I had in mind. Reckon somebody must have overheard Webb talking to me there in the hotel lobby, but I sure don't call to mind anybody hanging around close right then. Oh, well, no harm done. I got a couple of black eyes and a cut lip out of it, but I did have some fun. That hellion Doran must have put in some time in the prize ring, to learn to swing his fists like he did. But their cute little scheme didn't pan out as figured, so what the hell!"

Brant rode swiftly, more swiftly than he had intended during the latter part of his journey. Across the forks of the Canadian, and across the Prairie Dog fork of the Red, with the limitless plains of the Texas Panhandle stretching on all sides, until before him was the strange and wonderful cleft across the plains known as the Palo Duro Canyon.

The canyon, really a great sunken valley, was many miles wide and very deep. In places its rock walls were sheer, in others they were slopes of crumbling shale and rock fall. Shadowy, mysterious, well watered, with stands of cedar and other growth, it lay like the raw wound left in the rangeland by a random stroke of some flaming sword of vengeance. It was an ideal range for cattle, fenced in by walls hundreds of feet high. It had off-sets, such as Tule Canyon, where once more than fifty thousand head of wild mustangs ranged. When Charles Goodnight, the great Panhandle cat-tle baron, settled his cows in Palo Duro Canyon, he had to run buffalo from the range.

Brant rode along the rim of the canyon. Finally, in the distant southwest wall, he saw a dark and sinister looking opening choked with a bristle of cedars that grew thickest along the shadowy bat-tlements that hemmed it in. Far up the ominous gorge a mighty spire of naked rock soared above the stony walls. Veined and ledged and turreted, it had the appearance of a great lighthouse stand-ing isolated and alone, its lofty summit as devoid of life as it had been since the beginning of time.

It was a grim and even sinister formation, but to Austin Brant it was a friendly beacon welcom-ing the traveller home.

Brant skirted the west end of the canyon, crossed Palo Duro Creek and, just as dusk man-tled the prairie in its mystic robe, he reached the Running W ranchhouse.

After doing full justice to a bountiful surroundin' Brant stood on the ranchhouse porch gazing across the star burned prairie; endeavoring to envision something of the future of this vast land of wide spaces and unlimited opportunity. Unlike many of the older cowmen who took it for granted that present conditions would always prevail, Brant sensed that changes were coming to the grass-lands, that new forces were gathering, new events were in the making.

Nor was he wrong in his guess. Already the change was under way. Nesters and farmers were arriving. Cowboys were taking up spots of land and running their own brands. Soon the supremacy of the great cattle barons would be challenged, and out of that challenge would come conflict.

Some years before, Colonel Charles Goodnight had formed a partnership with Adair, an Irishman, who invested $375,000 as against Goodnight's Palo Duro ranch, the JA. The Prairie Cattle Company, the Spurs, the Matadors, and other organizations were buying land and running in great numbers of long-horns. The XIT, owned by the Capitol Syndicate, for many years the greatest ranch in America, was in process of formation. The XIT, when the deal to build the Texas State Capitol in exchange for land grants was consummated, would consist of three million acres—"Ten Counties in Texas!"

As yet the change had little affected the region wherein lay John Webb's Running W spread.

"But we're due to catch it, and before long," Brant mused as he gazed across the broad acres which Webb owned, or laid claim to.

Brant's first chore the following day was to visit Wes Morley of the Bar M and hand him the sum of money needed to meet his note. Morley evinced surprise.

"What's eatin' that old pelican?" he demanded. "I was in no hurry for this dinero. My note isn't due for nigh onto a month, and I could get an extension if I needed it, I figger."

Brant was not particularly surprised at this information. It but confirmed his suspicion that Webb had desired to get him away from Dodge City at once.

"And he came nigh to heading me into a worse rukus," he chuckled to himself as he rode back to the Running W. "That one has still got me puzzled. How in blazes did Doran learn I was packing that money!"

The mystery was intriguing, but Brant had other things to think about.

"We been havin' trouble—everybody's been havin' trouble," the temporary range boss left in charge of the spread told him. "We've been losin' cows, and so has everybody else. There's been brand blottin' and brand alterin', and we ain't been able to prove anything on anybody."

Brant nodded, his face grave. He understood very well the situation that was developing. It was a country where a cow thief could hole up easily and do a lucrative business in other men's cattle. In fact, the bonanza cattle days were at hand all over the West. It cost a dollar to drive a Texas steer to the Northern market. By the change of location, its value was increased four dollars. With such a margin of profit, anyone could make a fortune in cows, if he could manage to get hold of enough cows.

Matching wits on the part of the range rider and the widelooper became an exciting and often dangerous game, the one endeavoring to get evidence of guilt, the other to escape proof. Later would come the question of the relative rights of the big outfits and the small cattlemen. This controversy would also prove profitable for the rustler, who played both ends against the middle.

"It's them sidewinders from over New Mexico way what are responsible for most of the hell raisin'," the range boss declared.

"Chances are," Brant conceded. "But the home grown variety aren't doing so bad by themselves, either, I've a notion. We've got to do a heap of patrolling if we want to keep our beefs."

Brant determined on some patrolling on his own account, with a particular objective in view. The following morning found him riding north by east, toward the Bar O range. It was the spread owned by old Nate Loring, the Oklahoma cowman he had met in the Deadfall. Brant rode at a good pace, noting the position of various bunches of cows, estimating their numbers and checking his observations against conditions prevailing before he left for the northern drive. About midmorning found him traversing a section of rolling land dotted with thickets and occasional groves. To his left, some hundreds of yards distant, was a thick bristle of growth that fringed a wide and deep gulley, its steep sides grown with grass and flowering weeds. As far as the eye could reach it wound its uneven way across the prairie.

Smoke was taking it easy up the long slope of a rise when Brant suddenly stiffened in the saddle. From somewhere ahead came the hard, metallic clang of a rifle shot.

Instantly Brant was very much on the alert. That abrupt burst of gunfire might mean nothing—a range rider shooting at a coyote, perhaps—but again it might mean a good deal. With things as they were at present on the rangeland, most anything was liable to happen.

As he listened intently for further shots, a low drumming sound reached Brant's ears, which he quickly catalogued as the beat of a horse's irons on the farther side of the ridge.

"Comin' fast," he muttered. "Sounds like some jigger has places to go. Here he comes!"

Over the crest of the rise appeared a small bay horse, materializing against the skyline as if jerked up by unseen strings. Down the sag it scudded, as if blown before the wind. It was not headed straight for the Running W foreman but was veering sharply to the west.

"What in blazes?" Brant asked himself. "If that jigger doesn't pull up, he'll find himself at the bottom of that draw with a busted neck. Wonder what he's runnin' from?"

On came the fleeing rider, hunched over in the saddle. Suddenly Brant swore aloud. He had caught a glimpse of tossing, wind-blown curls back of the bay's head.

"For the love of Pete!" he exclaimed, "A girl!" His voice let loose in a stentorian roar—

"Look out! Pull up! Want to bust your neck?"

The rider of the bay apparently did not hear him, or if she did she took no heed. Brant swore again. His voice rang out, urgent, compelling—

"Trail, Smoke, trail!"

The great moros shot forward, angling to the left in obedience to the pressure of the rein on his neck. His irons beat a drumroll of sound from the hard earth. He slugged his head above the bit. His legs drove backward like steel pistons as he fairly poured his long body over the ground. Brant let out another shout of warning. But the girl on the bay did not slacken speed. The bay, apparently frantic with fright, sped on blindly, straight for the ominous fringe of growth that bordered the unseen gulch.

Brant was also headed for the gulch. The

course of the two riders formed a triangle, its apex the bristle of low brush. Brant's eyes narrowed. He twisted the split reins together and dropped them on Smoke's neck. He saw now that the girl was sawing frantically at the bay's bridle, and getting no results.

"Hellion's got the bit in his teeth," Brant muttered, "and he's scared blind loco about something. This is going to be close."

On raced the moros, without slackening speed, as the growth and the lip of the draw seemed to fairly leap toward them. Brant gripped Smoke's swelling barrel hard with his thighs. He rammed his feet deep into the stirrups. The bay was almost within arms' reach now, and almost to the first straggle of brush. Brant caught a glimpse of the girl's face, a white blur beneath her flying hair. Brant rose in his stirrups. Then he hurled himself sideways as shifted metal glinted in the sunlight.

There was a flash of fire, the roar of a shot. Brant gasped as a bullet burned its way along his ribs. He lunged forward, knocking the gun up even as the girl pulled trigger a second time. The slug fanned his face as the gun went spinning through the air. And just as the bay hit the brush with a crackling crash, Brant wound an arm about the girl's waist and jerked her from the saddle. The bay horse, with an almost human scream, went over the lip of the gorge and hurtled downward.

The girl struck at Brant with little fists, clawed at his face with her nails.

"Stop it, you hellcat!" he bellowed as Smoke hit the brush like a tornado, cleared the lip of the gorge in a great bound and came down on the slope on bunched hoofs.

By a miracle of agility, the blue horse kept his footing. Down the dizzy slope he scudded, apparently walking on empty air most of the time. Brant crushed the struggling girl against his breast with a force that squeezed most of the breath out of her body. Brant seized the bridle from Smoke's neck and steadied him. Smoke went over a bench like a flickering blue sunbeam, sailed through the air and landed on the slope a dozen feet farther down with a jolt that nearly drove Brant's spine through the top of his head.

"Settin' on his tail," Smoke took the last score of yards in a blaze of glory and a cloud of dust. An avalanche of loosened pebbles and boulders went along with him. They hit the bottom of the gorge together. The boulders kept going for some distance. Smoke skittered to a slithering halt and stood snorting and blowing.

Brant loosened his grip on the gasping girl. He glared down at her, his temper not improved by the sting of the bullet sear along the ribs and the uncomfortable warm stickiness that accompanied it.

"What's the big notion?" he demanded wrathfully. "I risk getting myself scattered all over the prairie to save you from getting your neck busted and you throw at me and try to claw my eyes out. I—"

Abruptly he ceased speaking. He stared incredulously at the piquant little face that seemed to be all great terrified blue eyes.

"He—heck and blazes!" he exclaimed. "I know you. You're the girl I saw in the Deadfall, up at Doran's Crossing on the Cimarron!"

Chapter Eight

Some of the fear left the girl's eyes. "And—and I know you," she said. "You're the cowboy who had the fight there. You're—you're Austin Brant!"

"That's right," Brant replied. "And you're Verna Loring, old Nate's niece. Say, what in blazes is going on hereabouts? What's the notion, skalleyhootin' around over the prairie like you were trying to outrun your shadow, and throwin' down on folks? And what was that shooting about over the other side of the sag?"

"If—if you'll just let me breathe—a little—I'll try and tell you," Verna Loring gasped in reply.

Brant suddenly realized he was still holding her much tighter than the occasion now warranted. He colored beneath his tan, loosening his hold. Swinging down lithely from the saddle, he set her on her feet. She swayed slightly, and he slid his arm back around her slim waist to steady her. He noted absently that her curly head came barely to his shoulder.

"Feel better?" he asked anxiously. "Aren't hurt any way, are you?"

"No, I'm not hurt," she replied. "You just about squeezed the life out of me, that's all."

"Had to do something," Brant grinned. "That

is, if I wanted to keep any hide on my face. You were giving me a right smart going over."

"I'm sorry," Verna said contritely, "but I was so terribly frightened. I thought you were another of those men."

"What men?"

"The men who shot at me."

"Shot at you! You mean to tell me some sidewinder took a shot at a woman!"

"I don't think they realized I was a woman," Verna replied. "My hat was pulled down over my hair, and I wasn't very close to them. It fell off when my horse ran away."

"Uh-huh, you do look sort of like a boy in those overalls—from a distance," Brant admitted. "Sort of cute, though."

Verna blushed and hurried on with her story.

"I was taking a ride this morning," she said. "I rode farther from the ranchhouse than I ever did before. Over the other side of that hill I saw two men beside a little fire. There was a calf or a young cow lying on the ground near them. They were doing something to it."

"Blotting or altering a brand, the chances are," Brant interrupted grimly.

"I don't know," the girl replied. "But when I rode toward them, one of them waved his hat at me."

"Uh-huh," Brant remarked, even more grimly, "wavin' you 'round! When a cow thief is at a fire, working over a brand or running a brand and a jigger comes riding along, he waves his hat in a half-circle from left to right, that means 'stay the heck away from here if you don't want to stop hot lead!' Then what happened?"

"I thought it was a couple of our boys," Verna said. "I kept on riding toward them, and one of them shot at me. The bullet struck my horse. He squealed and jumped and nearly threw me. Then he whirled around and ran. I tried to stop him, but couldn't. I couldn't do a thing with him. Then I saw you riding toward me and I was terribly frightened. I had the pistol Uncle Nate told me to carry so I drew it and fired at you."

"Uh-huh, so I noticed," Brant nodded dryly, caressing his sore ribs.

"I'm sorry," the girl said contritely, "terribly sorry. The bullet didn't strike you, did it?"

"Nothing to pay any mind to," Brant returned lightly. "But if it had been a couple of inches to the right, well, I reckon you would have gone down that cutbank along with your horse."

"And I haven't even thanked you for saving my life," Verna exclaimed remorsefully.

"Was a plumb pleasure," Brant returned. "I'd like to have the chore of doing it every day."

"Well, I wouldn't like to go through the experience, every day," Verna declared with feeling. "My poor horse. I'm afraid he is killed."

" 'Pears like it," Brant replied, glancing toward the sprawled brown shape a little ways up the draw. "I'll take a look. Want to get your saddle off, anyhow."

He walked to where the horse lay. A little later he returned, carrying the saddle and bridle.

"Busted his neck," he said. "It was a good thing, though. Chances are you would have had to shoot him. He was bad hurt. That slug hit him in the flank." His eyes were coldly gray as he spoke, his face bleak.

"I'd sure like to line sights with those sidewinders," he said. "If that slug had been a little higher—" he broke off without finishing the sentence. But Verna Loring understood what was implied, and shuddered. She glanced up fearfully at the growth fringed lip of the draw.

"You—you don't think they might come—looking for us?" she asked.

"Wish they would—I'd like to get a look at them," Brant replied. "No chance, though. Reckon they hightailed in a hurry as soon as they slid their ropes off that critter. Well, I've a notion this draw peters out up to the north and we can get topside again. Reckon we might as well be moving."

He lashed Verna's rig behind his own saddle. Then he mounted Smoke and held the girl in front of him. Smoke offered no objections to the double load and Verna appeared content to travel that way. Brant was eminently satisfied with the arrangement and let Smoke take his time. With the result that it was well along in the afternoon when they at last reached the Bar O ranchhouse.

Old Nate Loring gave Brant a warm welcome. He swore luridly when acquainted with the day's happenings.

"I'm beginnin' to wonder if I was so smart, after all, to come to this section," he growled. "Oklahoma was gettin' bad enough, but this 'pears to be worse and gettin' no better fast. There was a bad shootin' over to town the other night. Two jiggers planted in Boot Hill and another one in a bad way."

Brant nodded soberly. "I'm afraid this is just the beginning," he said. "We're in for more trouble, and soon. The ranges are too crowded down in the skillet. The Panhandle is the natural outlet. They're headed this way from the Brazos country, from the Nueces, the Trinity, the Colorado rainsheds. Right now the real big spreads are in central and south Texas. But soon the Panhandle is going to see such outfits as have never been known in Texas before. Things are going to boom, but it isn't going to last. Nesters and small owners and homesteaders and grangers are already beginning to come. More and more of them will come. The big spreads will be cut up into farms and townships. And everywhere you look there'll be wire."

"You really believe it?" old Nate asked, skeptically.

"Yes," Brant replied, "I do. The oldtimers don't. They say the grassland will never change. They're wrong. The change is taking place right under their noses, only they can't see it. But in the end it'll be a change for the better. There'll be law and order, homes, better cows, and better markets. But there'll be hell a-plenty first."

Old Nate shook his grizzled head. He glanced at his niece who was listening, wide-eyed.

"Scairt I shouldn't have brought you inter such a section, younker," he said.

"I'm glad you did," the girl returned sturdily. "This is a growing country, and I want to grow with it. I like it here."

"It's sure getting to be a nicer and nicer country to be in, all the time," Brant declared heartily. Old Nate chuckled. For some reason, Verna blushed.

Included among the comfortable furnishings of the Bar O ranchhouse was, to Brant's surprise, a small piano.

"Packed it all the way here by wagon," old Nate chuckled. "Verna insisted on bringin' it. Had one dickens of a time keepin' it from gettin' wet and spiled crossin' the rivers, but there she is, all roped and hawgtied. I'm goin' out to the kitchen to help the cook stir his stumps. Mebbe Verna'll play you some music."

So Verna Loring played for him, while the shadows lengthened, the sky flamed scarlet and gold above the western hills, and the hush of evening descended on the rangeland.

Brant declined a pressing invitation to spend the night at the Bar O.

"Want to be back at the spread in the morning," he told his host. "Lot of chores that need looking after."

He rode home beneath the stars, the rangeland a blue and silver mystery blanketed in silence. As he rode, he whistled gaily, or sang snatches of love songs in a voice that caused Smoke to flatten his ears and snort in abject dismay.

Chapter Nine

Brant had plenty to do. Among other things, he made a careful survey of the cows on the spread in order to ascertain the possibility of another trail herd without delay. In the course of this activity he learned things that caused his black brows to draw together.

"You're right, we're losing critters," he told his range boss. "More than I'd figured on. Not only calves, but a heap of prime beef critters. We've got to organize regular line riding, night and day. We can't afford the losses we're suffering. I sure wish the Old Man and the rest of the boys would get back pronto."

A week later, much to Brant's relief, old John Webb and the outfit roared into camp.

"Everything went hunky-dory," said Webb after he and Brant had shaken hands. "I got a sight more for the remuda than I'd hoped for. Shanghai Pierce sure did me a good turn. Incidentally, he sent regards to you. A nice feller, old Shang."

Brant was counting noses. He missed a familiar face.

"Where's Cole Dawson?" he asked abruptly.

Webb shrugged his big shoulders. "Damned if I know," he replied. "He came to me the morning you rode out of town and asked for his time. Said he calc'lated to stick around Dodge for a spell. Said he might have a try at buffalo hunting for a change. Ain't seen him since. Just as well. He's been on the prod for quite a while, and he sure wasn't better at all after you hauled him out of the Cimarron at the Crossin', and then saved his hide in Dodge. Feller would think you'd handed him a dirty deal of some sort, instead of savin' his wuthless carcass. He's a queer jigger."

"But a mighty good cowman," Brant interjected.

"Uh-huh," agreed Webb, "but I can get plenty of them without havin' to put up with Cole's loco notions. I'm glad he drew his wages. By the way, speakin' of pesky critters, I saw that big feller Doran up at the Crossin', the one they say owns the Deadfall. He was in a helluva shape. All stove up. Had one arm in a sling and was walkin' with a cane."

"Must have fallen down and hurt himself," Brant commented.

"Uh-huh," Webb returned dryly, "off a cliff, from the looks of him."

Another busy week followed. Brant had plenty to do, but he did manage to find time to drop in at the Bar O ranchhouse a couple of times. Old Nate was glad to see him, and Verna did not appear particularly displeased. One day Nate Loring rode part of the way back to the Running W with his young friend. In the course of the ride, Nate discussed something that caused Brant to do some serious thinking. They were inspecting a bunch of Loring's longhorns, estimating their weight for possible shipping.

"There's too much length and bone in those darn critters," Loring remarked. "You don't get the meat off their carcasses you should, and meat is what brings in the money. Reminds me of somethin' up in Oklahoma. A feller up there from back East owns a little spread. Bought it when he came west. Raised critters up in New England, he said. Well, that feller, Tom Sutton, sent back East for some bulls like what he used to handle there. He called 'em Herefords. Well, he crossed them Herefords with Longhorn cows and them crosses showed a weight of three hundred pounds and better more than critters from a scrub bull. That feller had a notion. Might work down here, if a jigger could just get the bulls. But them Herefords don't travel well over rough country—their hoofs won't take it. Reckon folks hereabouts will hafta wait until the railroads come along before they try anything like that."

Brant nodded, his eyes thoughtful. "You happen to know that feller?" he asked.

"Uh-huh," Loring replied, "know him well. Nice feller."

"Reckon he has quite a few of those Hereford bulls on hand by now."

"Uh-huh, reckon he has. He brought them in and some other bulls he called Galloways. Kept his pure stock bunch up that way."

Brant nodded again, but did not pursue the conversation. He had already learned, in the course of talks with Loring, from just where in Oklahoma the old man originated.

Another busy week followed. Then, one morning, John Webb received some disquieting news.

"A nester's moved in down on the southwest

range," one of his line riders informed Webb. "He's shoved in a big herd and is buildin' a ranchhouse. Got a salty lookin' bunch of hands with him."

Webb let out a roar of rage. He summoned Austin Brant and half a dozen of his most trustworthy hands.

"We'll just see about this," he raged as they saddled up. "No blankety-blank nester is goin' to squat on my range. I got enough troubles without that. Come on, you hellions, stir your stumps. We got things to do."

South by west they rode, at a fast clip. As they drew nearer the location in question, a peculiar sound reached their ears, coming from beyond a long straggle of thicket they were paralleling. It was a metallic whining and creaking, punctuated by a rhythmic clicking which Brant soon catalogued as the ring of axes on wood. They rounded the thicket and came upon a scene of great activity.

Over to the left was a fairly deep and narrow canyon, one of the many off-shoots of the Palo Duro. From its wooded depths came the clang of axes. On the near lip were clustered a number of men.

"Cutting timber down in the gulch and bringing it to the surface with wire pulleys," Brant said. "Look, there goes a wagonload now."

Rumbling across the prairie some distance ahead was a huge wagon drawn by eight horses. It was loaded with newly cut logs. Even as the Running W outfit drew near, a ponderous log came dangling up the canyon wall at the end of a long cable drawn by a windlass on the lip of the gorge.

"No sod huts for that jigger, whoever he is,"

Brant apostrophised the nester. "He's going in for a regular casa. Means business."

"I'll business him!" growled old John, glaring at the workers on the canyon lip, who had paused from their labors and were silently watching the approaching troop.

Brant said nothing. He had an uneasy premonition that Webb might run into considerable difficulty in the process of "businessing" the unknown nester.

The Running W bunch did not pause at the scene of operations on the canyon lip.

"They're just hired hands—no use argifyin' with them," Webb said. "I want to do my talkin' to the jigger responsible for this."

Following the course taken by the wagon, they rode on. Soon they sighted a low rise whereon grew scattered trees. On the crest of this rise the walls of a ranchhouse were already rising. Webb snorted like a steer tangled in a cactus patch. He quickened the pace of his horse. In a compact body the Running W outfit charged up the hill.

As they drew near, they noted two men sitting their horses a little to one side of some construction and watching their approach. One was a huge man, massive with the solid massiveness of a granite block. His companion was slender and sat his magnificent bay horse with the natural grace accentuated by a lifetime in the saddle. Brant suddenly uttered an exclamation. Old John swore under his mustache as they pulled up within a dozen paces of the motionless pair.

"Cole Dawson!" Webb bellowed. "Where in blazes did you come from? And what are you doin' here, Kane?"

It was Norman Kane who replied, an amused note in his musical voice. "Gettin' my spread in shape," he replied.

"Gettin' *your* spread in shape!" bawled Webb. "Are you the hellion nestin' down here?"

"Reckon I'm the hellion you're talkin' about," Kane returned imperturbably, "but I don't get the nester part of it. What do you mean?"

"What do I mean!" roared the irate Running W owner. "This is my range you're on."

"Don't think so," Kane returned. "I got a notion it's mine."

Old John turned purple and breathed with apparent difficulty. Norman Kane appeared to take no notice of these alarming symptoms. He nodded cordially to Brant.

"How are you, fellow?" Kane inquired. "Glad to see you made it back all right."

Old John broke in. "Kane," he stormed, "I'm tellin' you to get your truck and your cows off my land."

"Webb, it is not your land," Norman Kane replied evenly. "It never was your land. It has always been federal land—open range. I have leased this section, and I expect to get complete title before long. Want to see the papers?"

"Damn you," sputtered Webb, "I've run my cows on this range for thirty years, and my Dad run his on it before me!"

"And neither of you took the trouble to get title to it," Kane replied imperturbably. "By the way, have you got title to the rest of your holdin's, other than your north range, where your ranchhouse is? If you haven't, take a little friendly advice and hustle to do it. There'll be other folks headed this way before you know it. Don't get caught settin' again, Webb."

Webb was about to make a hot reply, but Austin Brant laid a restraining hand on his angry Boss's arm.

"Hold it, John," he cautioned. "If he's telling us straight, and I figure he is, there's not a thing you can do. No sense in rarin' and chargin'. We're outsmarted, and that's all there is to it."

Webb set his mouth hard, mastering himself by an effort. "The round-up ain't over till the last brand's run," he growled.

Brant was eying Cole Dawson with a speculative gaze. "I see now," he remarked, "why you two jiggers had your heads together there in the Deadfall. So Cole lined you up on conditions down here, Kane?"

"Damn double-crosser!" exploded Webb.

"I got the first double-cross," Dawson returned truculently. "Why didn't you give me the foreman's job like I had it comin', 'stead of handin' it to that sprout? I can hand back what's handed to me, anytime. I'm on my own now, Webb, and workin' for a man who appreciates me."

Norman Kane's perfectly formed lips quirked slightly at the corners, but he made no remark. Old John snorted, glared at Dawson, and abruptly whirled his horse.

"C'mon, let's get out of here, before I bust a cinch," he told his men.

Brant lingered a moment as the others rode away. Kane nodded to him again in friendly fashion.

"Hope there's no hard feelin's, Brant," he said.

"Not over this deal," Brant replied. "It's just a

matter of business. Webb got caught setting, that's all." He started to ride after the others when a thought suddenly struck him.

"By the way," he remarked, "did you stop at the Deadfall on your way back to Oklahoma?"

Kane's eyes narrowed slightly. The steely glitter in their black depths seemed to suddenly intensify.

"Why, yes," he replied. "Why?"

"Oh, nothing," Brant returned easily. "I was just wondering if Phil Doran was enjoying good health when you left."

Without waiting for an answer, he whirled Smoke and cantered after Webb and the hands. Norman Kane set perfectly motionless in his saddle, staring after Brant. Cole Dawson had to speak twice before he attracted his attention.

Old John had cooled considerably by the time they got back to the ranchhouse, but he was still far from a good temper.

"I'll even up with that hellion if it's the last thing I do," he declared. "And that blankety-blank Cole Dawson! I wish you had let the horned toad drown, or get hung!"

"Cole's just a dumb shorthorn," Brant returned. "I don't figure there's any real bad in him. He went on the prod because he figured he got a raw deal. He's like a little boy who busts his toy wagon because it turns over. But let's forget all that for the time being. What you want to do is get busy and make sure of your title to the outlying lands you've been using all this time. What happened today is just the beginning. I've been telling you a long time that things are going to change. You laughed at me, but right now you've had an example of what's in store for the Panhandle open range. Get busy, Uncle John, you can't afford to take chances."

"Reckon you're right," Webb conceded. "I don't know what the world's comin' to. Gettin' so an honest man can't figger to make an honest livin'. Why can't them hellions of nesters and two-cow-and-a-bull owners stay where they belong!"

"Perhaps there ain't any place for them to stay," Brant replied gently. "After all, they're just looking for a chance to live and enjoy life a mite. Reckon it isn't just right to refuse them the chance, Uncle John. When everything is considered, folks like you and I have had it pretty soft. Having it soft sometimes makes folks get hard. They shut their own front door and say the whole world's warm. It isn't, Uncle John. It's mighty cold outside for some folks. Maybe it won't be a bad notion to open the door a mite and let some other folks in where it's warm."

Old John stared at his young foreman. He tugged his mustache, rumbling in his throat. John Webb was far from being a bad man, but he was set in his ways. He had been brought up to look upon the conditions he knew as proper conditions. He lived within his own narrow sphere of influence, and lived largely in the past. Austin Brant, on the contrary, had the vision of youth, the broader understanding that came from travel, better education, and closer contact with his fellow-men. To him the Panhandle, Oklahoma, Kansas were all pieces of his native land and its people were all his fellow Americans.

Old John sensed this dimly, and there was a grudging admiration in the glance he bent upon Brant, though he still strove to look combative.

"We'll see about it. We'll see about it!" he growled.

Brant permitted himself an inward smile. He understood his Boss, and knew that this truculent growl was really a concession on Webb's part, an admission that there might be two sides to the question, and that both might be worthy of consideration. Webb's next remark confirmed the opinion.

"I'll do as you say," he grunted. "I'll get in touch with the land office right away and protect myself. As for Kane, I hope he sets down on a tarantuler. To hell with him!"

But subsequent developments caused Webb to say some sulphurous things about the Flying V owner.

"The hellion's fencin' his land," a line riding puncher told. Webb not long after his conversation with Brant. "They're cuttin' posts down in that canyon, haulin 'em up and settin' 'em, and stringin' bob wire on 'em."

"The next thing we know, the sidewinder will be runnin' in sheep!" roared Webb. "Bob wire fence in the Panhandle!"

"You'll see plenty of barbed wire fence in this section before long," Austin Brant predicted. "The big new spreads will be going in for it heavy. Particularly if they start improving their breed of cows."

Brant was eminently right in his prophecy. Soon the great XIT spread would put up more than eight hundred miles of fence to enclose the ranch's vast domain, at a cost of more than $175,000. Cross fences would increase the mileage to fifteen hundred.

"And speaking about improving breeds," Brant remarked, "there's something I want to take up with you. I see a chance for the Running W to get the jump on every outfit in this section, even Goodnight and his JA."

He recounted his conversation with Nate Loring. Webb was interested, but pointed out objections.

"You could never bring them breed bulls all the way here from Oklahoma," he reminded. "They couldn't make the march over the rough ground. Their hoofs wouldn't take it. A longhorn is equipped pertickler for hard goin', but them blood critters has got soft from ablin' around over easy pastures."

"I've got a notion how it could be done," Brant replied. "I figure it's worth trying, anyhow."

"We'll talk about it again after we get the next herd ready for the north drive," Webb decided. "Right now, the big chore is to get them cows ready for the trail."

Others beside Webb had things to say about Norman Kane's fencing project. There were some small owners occupying range directly south of Kane's holdings. When Kane finished his fencing, these owners realized that their cows were cut off from the water. Naturally they didn't take kindly to the new conditions. Their criticism of Kane was bitter. They did more than criticize. Kane's wire was cut in a number of places. He repaired the breaks and set men riding to guard the fences. Shootings from ambush followed next. There was the making of a first class range war under way.

"Looks like the hellion is goin' to get his

comeuppance without any moves on our part," John Webb chuckled, when informed of the troubles besetting his unwanted neighbor.

Austin Brant, however, took another view of the matter. "If it's bad for him, it's bad for us, too," Brant declared. "There's the making of plenty of trouble for everybody in this. All of a sudden we've got the honest 'little fellow' siding with the wideloopers and brand blotters. And this is only the beginning. With more wire coming there'll be more trouble coming. Something has to be done."

"What?" countered Webb. "Those jiggers down there can't get their cows to water, and if the cows can't get water, they can't hold on. Which means the little fellers are goin' to be ruined. They ain't gonna take it layin' down. If Kane insists on keepin' his fences up, what can anybody do about it?"

"I've got the answer, if I can make Kane listen to sense," Brant replied. "I'm going to take a chance on riding over to see him soon and putting a proposition up to him."

While Brant was debating how best to approach the Flying V owner, Norman Kane proceeded to play into his hands by kicking up a row that gave even *him* pause.

One morning there appeared on a wall of the Tascosa post office, and in other places, a notice printed in heavy black type:

A FAIR WARNING

Anyone hereafter meddling with my wire will be risking death or serious injury. I am a law abiding citizen, but have received little protection from the law. Therefore I have taken measures to protect my property from the depredations of the lawless.

Heed this warning or pay the price!

(Signed) Norman Kane
Owner, Flying V Ranch

The notice was hotly debated in various gathering places that included general stores and saloons. Some held that Kane was justified in taking extreme measures. His wire had been cut; his men shot at. Others maintained that taking the law in your own hands is a bad business and likely to get you in trouble. The discussions raged furiously and didn't tend to improve conditions that were already far from good.

There was much conjecture as to just what Kane had done to protect his property. Curiosity rose to a high pitch. Everybody was talking about the matter and making gusses, most of them decidedly farfetched.

Slim Lubbock and Bull Soderman, two of Wes Morley's Bar M riders, were discussing the subject over glasses of red-eye in a Tascosa saloon. The hour was late, the likker potent, and Slim and Bull had been going it strong for most of the night.

"I shay," remarked Slim, with owlish gravity, "what we should do ish ride over there and find out how he's got that darn bobsh wire fixed so it'll take care of itself."

"We ain't got no cutters," Bull objected.

"Oh, we won't do any cuttin'—that getsh you in trouble,' replied Slim. "We'll just look 'em over, careful like. Find out whatsh al 'bout."

Bull was still a bit doubtful as to the wisdom of

the move, but Slim finally carried the day. They left the saloon together, rather shakily, and managed to unhitch and fork their horses. Once in the saddle, life-long habit asserted itself and they had no trouble staying there.

Slim was little and scrawny and liable to be cantakerous. Bull was big, beefy, good-natured. Both were tophands and well liked.

It was quite a ride to the Flying V wire, but they made it without mishap. They were more sober when they got there than when they started, but not enough to alter their decision. They were still determined to learn what Norman Kane was up to. The full moon was shining brightly in a clear sky, bathing the prairie in silvery light. The taut strands of rusty wire gleamed palely golden. The fence posts marched in a seemingly endless line.

Although still more than half drunk, Solderman and Lubbock had sense enough to choose what appeared to be a safe spot to approach the fence. There was no growth within hundreds of yards, no place where a fence guard could hole up with ready rifle. If someone was watching from afar, the two cowhands felt they'd have such a head start that distancing possible pursuit would not be difficult. They rode up to a hundred feet of the fence, gave the whole terrain a careful once-over and dismounted. They approached the wire with caution, not touching it at first. Then, emboldened by the deserted silence, they began a more thorough examination, tugging at the strands, shaking posts.

"Hey!" suddenly called Slim, who was some twenty feet behind his companion. "Here's a post that ain't in the ground. Just hangin' loose. Bottom end sawed off. I can pull it way up and—"

Bull Solderman never knew what more Slim intended saying. There was a crashing roar, a yellowish flare that dimmed the moonlight. Bull was knocked end over end by the force of the blast. He lay for a moment, stunned, deafened and blinded. When he scrambled to his feet he was cold sober.

The sawed-off post, still stapled to the wire, sagged drunkenly over a gaping hole in the ground from which rose trickels of smoke and a smell of burned dynamite. Slim Lubbock lay some distance from the smoking crater, his face covered with blood, one leg twisted grotesquely. He was unconscious and moaning softly. Horrified and still dazed, Solderman ran to him.

"Slim! Slim!" he called inanely. "You all right?"

Slim was far from being all right. Bull realized that as his vision cleared and he dropped a loop on his scattered senses.

The horses had dashed away when the blast went off. Now they stood a hundred yards distant, snorting and stamping. Bull whistled and the well trained animals came to his call. A powerful man, he managed to fork his cayuse with Slim cradled in his arms. He rode madly away from the scene of horror.

It was many miles to the Bar M ranchhouse and Bull knew that Slim was badly in need of medical attention. On the other hand, the Running W casa was but a couple of miles distant. Bull headed for the Running W. He arrived there as the sky was graying with dawn. His yells brought the hands tumbling from the bunkhouse and Webb and Austin Brant onto the porch of the Bull Mansh.

Brant immediately took charge. He carried Slim's unconscious form into the house and placed him on a couch. He ordered a hand to saddle up and ride to Tascosa for a doctor. Then he and Webb did a little rough surgery on Slim.

"He's considerably bunged up, but I think he'll make it," Brant finally said. "That leg fracture isn't compounded, and the head cuts aren't very deep. Doesn't seem to be any skull fracture. I can't say about concussion. He may just be out from shock. We've done all we can and will have to wait for the doctor. And now, Bull, tell us what happened."

Solderman told them, with plenty of profanity. Brant listened in silence, his face darkening.

"I've heard of that trick before," he said when Bull had finished. "It was used down in Navarro County during the wire war along the Trinity. I think I know how it was worked, but I'd like to ride over to where that blast let off and make sure. It'll be daylight by the time we get there. Come along, Bull, and lead us to the spot. Half a dozen men come along, too. Want plenty of witnesses to what we find."

"What about those Flyin' V skunks," Bull asked, a little nervously, as they got under way. "Think they'll be waitin' there for us? They must have heard the racket at their ranchhouse."

"I think that's the last place you'll find any of the Flying V outfit right now," Brant replied. "Let's go."

Brant was right. When they reached the scene of the explosion, nobody was in sight. Brant gazed at the hole in the ground, above which the sawed-off post dangled. He pointed to the post.

"You'll notice there's a short section of wire fastened to the bottom end of that post," he remarked. "Now scatter out over the ground and see if you can find anything."

The cowboys dismounted and began poking about in the tall grass. A few minutes passed and one called, "Hey! here's part of an old muzzle-loadin' shotgun! The barrel's all busted to hell."

"Figured it would be," Brant observed. "Any wire fastened to the trigger?"

"Uh-huh, a little short piece."

Brant took the shattered weapon and turned it over in his hands.

"Tell you how it works," he said. "A plumb devilish contraption, and plumb simple and easy to make. You just take an old muzzle-loader and put in a charge of powder. Drop a dynamite cap down onto the charge of powder. Then fill the barrel with dynamite and cork it tight with a wooden plug. Fasten one end of a piece of wire to the trigger. The other end to the bottom of the post that isn't in the ground. Put a cap on the nipple and cock the gun, all ready for shooting. Then you put the gun in a wooden box, dig a shallow hole under the bottom of the post, put the box in the hole and cover it over with earth."

"But what if the hammer happens to drop while you're fooling with the darn thing?" a young puncher asked.

"You wouldn't even know it happened," Brant replied dryly. "The contraption is safe enough so long as the strands of fence wire are not tampered with. The wire between the bottom of the post and the trigger is a bit slack, so that a cow rubbing against the post won't set it off. But if the fence wire is cut, the sawed post falls over, the end kicks up, the trigger is pulled, the dynamite is set off and pieces of shotgun are scattered all over the county. And usually pieces of whover did the wire cutting. Slim Lubbock just had a drunk's luck, that's all."

The comments of the listening punchers were blistering, their opinion of Norman Kane and all he stood for not complimentary to *Senor* Kane, to say the least.

The story spread like wildfire, and there was merry hell to pay. It took all the argumentative powers of John Webb and Austin Brant to keep Wes Morley and the Bar M hands from riding to the Flying V and shooting it out. Even the larger spread owners, who had been rather inclined to go along with him, turned thumbs down on his fence bombs.

So when Austin Brant rode over with his proposition, Kane was in a mood to listen to anything that would lessen the tension between him and the small owners.

The chief bone of contention was a stream that ran south across Kane's range, turned sharply west not far from his south wire and plunged into a canyon. This stream had been the foremost watering place for stock owned by the small ranchers to the south and east. There were waterholes on the range, but these were scant and were steadily drying up. Soon the little fellows' situation would be precarious.

Kane was firm in his determination to keep his range fenced, but he was not pleased with the row he had kicked up. He listened to Brant when the latter submitted his plan.

After talking with Kane, Brant rode south and contacted the various small spread owners. As a result of his efforts, a truce was declared. Every available hand got busy with picks, shovels, plows and blasting powder. A channel was dug south from the stream. Into this was diverted a portion of the creek's water. Ditches were dug to the various waterholes. New holes were excavated. The immediate problem was solved.

With their stock no longer threatened with extermination, the ire of the small owners cooled somewhat. But there was still plenty of cussin' over the damned "bob" wire. The rusty strands with their bristling barbs were an affront to every believer in the open range. Horses and cows ran into the wire and suffered lacerations. These became infected with screw worms. Loss of stock resulted. The average cowhand regarded wire with about the same affection he would have lavished on a case of spotted fever.

"But there's no use trying to set back the clock," Austin Brant declared. "Wire is coming to the grass lands to stay. The time is coming when a jigger won't feel like he's in a city if he meets two men on the range in as many days. We've got to get used to changed conditions and regulate things accordingly. There's still plenty of room for everybody, but from now on it is the smart jigger who can see things as they are who is going to come out on top."

One day while the work of diverting the water was in progress, Brant ran into Cole Dawson. He was surprised at Dawson reining in his horse and holding up his hand for Brant to do likewise. Brant waited for Dawson to speak.

Cole scowled ferociously, but his voice was almost apologetic when he addressed his former range companion.

"Brant," he said, "I reckon you hate my guts, and maybe you got reason to, but I don't want you hatin' 'em for something I didn't do. I just want to tell you, I didn't have a damn thing to do with that dynamite bomb business. I talked against it."

"Not surprised to hear that you did, Cole," Brant replied. "No matter what you've done or haven't done, I can't see you pulling a sidewinder trick like that. As I said up in Dodge, when they accused you of shooting a jigger in the back, you just aren't made that way."

With a nod he rode on, leaving Dawson staring after him, a peculiar expression in his eyes. Dawson had been riding west toward the Flying V wire. Abruptly he turned his horse and rode due south, purposefully.

Shortly after the water diverting episode, Brant received some disquieting information anent the doings of *Senor* Kane. He learned that Kane was a frequent visitor at the Bar O ranchhouse. Finally one afternoon, the two young men arrived at the ranchhouse at the same time.

Kane and Brant were cordial to one another. Verna Loring was cordial to both. But just the same the situation was somewhat strained. For the first time in his life, Austin Brant learned what it meant to be ill at ease in another man's presence, and somewhat uncertain of himself. There was no denying Norman Kane's charm. His physical perfection was the least of it. He had an urbane manner, a gift for casual conversation. Every word and gesture bespoke his vivid personality. Brant was forced to admire him, his utter self-confidence, his equaly utter lack of self-consciousness. The highlight of the occasion came when Kane seated himself at the piano, ran his slender fingers powerfully across the keys, flung back his handsome head and sang, in a pure, sweet tenor, a hauntingly beautiful ballad of the range—

> When the moon shines down on the chaparral
> And the stars come out, one by one,
> While wan and gray are the pinons tall
> That stood so green 'neath the sun—
>
> There's a dream that comes from the yesteryears,
> As I ride down the trail, all alone,
> Of one I see through a mist of tears,
> A dream of you, my own! my own!
>
> Moon and stars together,
> Each shall do their part
> To bring to life again the dream
> That dwells within my heart!
>
> Sad was the parting,
> Long the trail and lone,
> That brings me back again to you,
> To you, my own! My own!

As the last golden echoes died to silence, Norman Kane turned, smiled his thin, fleeting smile, and stood up with lithe grace.

"Well, so long, folks," he said. "Got to be goin'. Want to make it to Tascosa by dark."

With a nod to Brant and another smile, he strode out. Norman Kane understood to the full of the value of making an effectual departure.

Brant and Verna Loring walked out onto the porch and watched him ride away.

"Verna," Brant said suddenly, "what do you think of that feller, anyhow?"

"Austin, I don't know," the girl replied frankly. "He draws me strangely, and at the same time repels me. There is something about him I can't understand. Perhaps it is his eyes that are responsible. In front, they are all light and warmth, but in the back it seems that granite walls rise up to hide something that—perhaps it is not good to look upon. At times I feel as if I could go to the ends of the earth with him, but at the same time I know I would always be—afraid!"

Brant said nothing, but stared across the rangeland with unseeing eyes. Verna laid a slim little hand on his arm.

"Austin," she said softly, "no woman would ever be afraid with you—anywhere!'

Before Brant could reply, she had slipped back into the house. He hesitated a moment, half turned, then strode abruptly to his horse.

Chapter Ten

The early fall roundup, in preparation for the final drives north before winter would close the trails, got under way. The cowmen of the section joined together to plan the work and choose a round-up boss. By an almost unanimous vote, this important chore was assigned to Austin Brant. As one oldtimer said, "He's a young feller, but he's got the savvy a lot of the older hands ain't never seemed to tie onto."

This highly important matter attended to, the roundup strategy and tactics were handed over to Brant. His word was law and he had the final say-so in all matters. The owners of the cows were as much under his orders as any cowhand or wrangler. There was only one man to whom even the all-powerful round-up boss was chary of getting too uppity with—the cook. That truculent and habitually bad-tempered individual was monarch of all he surveyed and, within limits, did pretty much as he pleased. If it is true that an army travels on its stomach, what is to be said of an outfit of hungry cowboys with some eighteen hours a day of gruelling toil on their hands? Cooks were in a class by themselves, and they knew it.

Brant's first chore was to choose trusted lieutenants who would be in charge of groups of hands that were to scour the range thoroughly in search of wandering cows, singly or in large groups. Brant "told off" his subordinates—gave them their orders—and the serious work of the roundup began.

The troops of cowboys rode out over the range and presently scattered until the hands were separated by distances that varied according to the type of range they were working. Coulees, canyons and brakes were combined for holed-up beefs and fugitive cows with late calves. The cattle were gathered up by ones and twos and small groups and driven to designated holding spots. At the holding spot, after the critters were held in close herd, the work of cutting out began. Various brands were segregated by driving the individual critters past a tally man who called and recorded the brands. The cow a calf was following was carefully noted and the calf branded the same as the mother.

With the greatest care, the beef cattle were cut and segregated according to brands. Those not wanted, the culls and cut-backs, were also separated to later be allowed to drift back onto the range, as were the calves and the cows not needed for shipment.

"I don't want any mavericks ambling around when this roundup is finished," Brant cautioned his men.

Several straymen representing distant spreads not included in the roundup, were present to drive home cows that had wandered far from their range. Each outfit gathered its beef cut together in readiness for the drive to market.

Dust and sweat and sun! The stench of burned hair and scorched flesh. Shouting and cursing. The whiz of ropes, the sizzle of the branding iron. The thud of horses' irons and the dull rumble of thousands of unshod hoofs. Sourdough biscuits, steaks fried in deep fat, numberless cups of steaming coffee. Then laughter and song and skylarking. The croon of the night-hawks, the rumbling of full-fed, contented cattle. The jingle of bridle irons and the popping of saddle leather in the velvety dark! Dreamless sleep beneath the stars! Round-up days!

The March of the Longhorns—the wildest, gayest, most carefree and most joyous phase of life the nation ever knew or ever will know. The March of the Longhorns! that exerted an influence hard to overestimate on the country over which it passed. It colored the tradition and the literature of a nation and hastened the spread of empire over a wild and untrodden land. For less than a score of years the vast panorama was painted on the dust clouds staining the sky and dimming the stars of the West, before it faded under the erasing hand of changing conditions. The cowboy was the plumed knight of the cactus and the mesquite, his armor denim and leather, his lance a whizzing length of three-eighths manila, his escutcheon the stamping of a glowing iron on hair and flesh, his sword a flaming sixgun wielded with unbelievable dexterity. He rode a crusade against the dumb, imponderable forces of nature, and, unlike the Crusaders of old, he rode triumphant, hat tilted, lips a-quirk, into the oblivion of a new era.

Norman Kane was an amused onlooker at the beginning of the roundup, but long before the first beef herd was driven to its home range, his own cows were rolling northward.

"Something to be said for wire," Brant observed to John Webb. "Does away with combing the whole range and cutting out."

Webb rumbled in his throat, but nevertheless looked thoughtful.

Under a hazy autumn sun the Running W shipping herd started on the long trek to Dodge City. Dust a-foggin', cowboys shouting, horses mettlesome and frisky, with bellowing and blatting and clashing horns the cows took the trail. The Canadian was crossed, and the tawny Red. Austin Brant rode with the herd, but when they reached the Cimarron he did not cross with the others. Instead with half a dozen chosen companions, he rode east, fording the river many miles farther on. After negotiating the crossing, they rode on east, veering somewhat to the north. Until, following the directions supplied Brant by old Nate Loring, they reached a small settlement called Cary. A few miles east of Cary, according to Loring, was the spread owned by Tom Sutton, the man who imported Hereford bulls to cross with his longhorn cows.

Brant located Sutton's spread without difficulty. He found Sutton to be an affable man who was willing to sell his surplus bulls. But Sutton voiced a word of warning.

"You'll never be able to run these critters back

to the Panhandle, son," he told Brant. "Their hoofs won't stand it over the rough ground. They'll be goin' lame on you before you reach the Cimarron and you'll end up by losin' every one of 'em. I'm glad of a chance to sell—got more than I got any use for now—but I don't want to take advantage of a feller, I tell you, you can't make it."

"I've got a notion," Brant replied. "See you have a blacksmith shop here."

"Uh-huh, a good one," Sutton replied, wonderingly.

"And I reckon I won't have any trouble buying all the shoes I want in Cary, eh?"

"No trouble at all," agreed the mystified rancher.

Next day the Oklahoma spread owner watched something the like of which he had never seen before. Shaking his head and muttering, he watched Brant and his hands nail iron shoes to the hooves of the bulls Brant had purchased. The word got around, and before the chore was completed a number of residents from town, and hands from nearby spreads formed an interested and skeptical audience. There were derisive remarks, much shaking of heads, and considerable outright laughter.

But when Austin Brant reached the Panhandle, although the Oklahoma gents were not there to see it, the laugh was on the other side of the face. The shod bulls plodded stolidly across the rough ground, and not a single one suffered lameness. Taking his time and making the trip by easy stages, Brant brought the herd intact to the Running W range.

The feat kicked up considerable excitement.

Men rode in from miles around to look over the prize animals and the iron that protected their tender hoofs.

"Son, you've started something," said Colonel Charles Goodnight of the JA spread, a speculative gleam in his fine eyes. "I figger the time will come when putting shoes on valuable beef critters will be a common practice."

Goodnight was a prophet not without honor in his own land, and this particular prognostication, along with others, proved to be sound.

Shortly after his return, Brant rode up to the Bar O. While Verna busied herself in the kitchen, Brant talked with old Nate in the living room.

"There's a new gamblin' hangout over in Tascosa," Loring remarked in the course of the conversation. "I understand she's a heller—up-to-date gamblin' riggin's, music, plate glass mirrors, gals, floods of likker. All first class. They're doing a big business. Heard they figgered first to squat at Clarendon, down toward the mouth of the Palo Duro, but Colonel Goodnight rode down and sort of persuaded the gamblin' gents to move on. There was quite a bit of cussin' and argifyin', I heard, but Goodnight is considerable of a feller and has a way with him when he sets out to *persuade* folks to do somethin'. Anyhow, the gamblers packed up and moved to Tascosa where folks don't 'pear to be so pertickler."

"Who opened it?" Brant asked.

"Feller who told me about it didn't know 'em," Loring replied. "Said they were new jiggers in the section. From up in Oklahoma, he believed. Said they were salty appearin' gents who know their business. Won't stand for any rough stuff. He said the games 'peared to be straight enough."

"Would be in the beginning, anyhow," Brant returned. "Reckon I'll have to drop in and look the place over the next time I'm in town. Figure to ride up in the next day or two."

Brant did ride to Tascosa two days later. He located the new place without difficulty and entered. Inside the door he paused, staring with astonishment. At the far end of the bar stood three men. One was Norman Kane. The other two were Phil Doran and Pink Hansen.

Kane noticed Brant's entrance, and walked over to the bar to join him in a drink.

"What you doing here, Kane?" Brant asked casually.

Norman Kane smiled his thin smile. "Got an interest in the diggin's," he replied.

"You have!"

"Uh-huh. I persuaded Doran and Hansen to come down to this section and open up. Put out the money for them to make the move on. They weren't doin' so well at the Crossin' anymore. Down here the place is a prime money maker. Good investment."

"If you don't mind investing in such a business," Brant conceded.

Kane's eyes narrowed a trifle. "Business is business," he returned composedly. "Where there's money to be took, I say take it."

Brant did not pursue the conversation further, but as he looked over the tables and noticed the cold-eyed, steel-nerved card sharps doing the dealing and manipulating, he had a feeling that there would be considerable "taking" in the Post-hole, as the place was named.

Kane finished his drink, nodded to Brant and strolled back to the far end of the bar. Neither Doran nor Hansen approached the Running W foreman, which was not surprising under the circumstances of their last meeting. Brant was conscious of their eyes hard upon him when he left the Posthole.

Chapter Eleven

When John Webb returned from the North drive, Brant had a serious conversation with the Running W owner.

"We're being robbed blind," he told Webb. "We didn't tally anything like the number of calves we should have at roundup, and we're losing steers and beefs off the range every day. I've got men riding line all the time, but still it goes on. Somebody is almighty slick about it."

"Them hellions from New Mexico!" growled Webb.

"Mebbe," Brant admitted, "but I'm beginning to wonder. I posted men where they'd have a mighty good chance to intercept any cows run in that direction, and so far they haven't seen a thing."

"How about them darn nesters down to the south, the little hellions you run water to after Kane fenced 'em out?"

"I can't say for sure," Brant admitted, "but if it's them, they're sure covering up."

"Trust 'em to do that," grunted Webb, with the big owner's habitual distrust of the little feller.

"Well, whoever is responsible, it's getting worse," Brant declared. "Never before have we lost so many cows as during the past few months."

It was not strange that Webb should ascribe most of his troubles to the New Mexico faction. In the shadow of the flat-topped mountains roamed bands of the most notorious killers and outlaws the West ever knew. They were made up of such men as William H. Boney (Billy the Kid), Frank McNab, Doc Skurlock, Charley Bowdre, Fred Waite, Tom O'Folliard, and other desperadoes. From all the frontier states and territories, particularly from Texas, outlaws, stage robbers, cow thieves, paid killers and other owlhoots had gathered to take part in the carnival of crime highlighted by such sanguinary episodes as the Lincoln County War. The well stocked ranches of the Panhandle offered rich pickings for those gentlemen of easy conscience and quick trigger finger. What Webb believed was equally believed by honest ranches all over the section. Even such a reputable cattleman as John Chisum was looked upon with suspicion by the Texas owners, because he happened to originate in New Mexico.

This condition furnished opportunity for homegrown wideloopers. With the blame for any outrage almost automatically placed upon the New Mexico owlhoots, the shrewd rustler of the Panhandle could get away with a lot and never be suspected. Many took advantage of this opportunity to fatten their herds with other men's cattle.

Austin Brant knew this, and while he did not discount the probability that the New Mexico owlhoots were doing the widelooping on the Running W, he did not overlook the possibility that the depredations might be credited to somebody closer to home.

Norman Kane was also having his troubles.

Several times within a two weeks period his wire was cut and his cows drifted out onto the Running W range. His hands, with the assistance of the Running W riders, herded them together and drove them back home.

"Chances are some more will still be maver-ickin' around," Kane told Brant. "I reckon you'll run onto 'em sooner or later."

Which proved to be the case. Quite a few more Flying V cows were encountered by the Running W cowboys and delivered to their proper owner.

"And each time my wire was cut, I lost quite a few head," Kane declared to John Webb. "Sure it's the New Mexico bunch. Who else? If I can just line sights with the hellions some time!"

Brant was thoughtful as he and Webb rode back to the ranchhouse.

"Funny, isn't it?" he remarked to the Boss. "They always cut Kane's east fence. Looks like they'd cut it on the west side, if it is the New Mexico owlhoots doing the widelooping."

"Can't never tell what an owlhoot is liable to do," Webb grunted. "And then again, mebbe it's them damn nesters down to the south what are re-sponsible. They would cut the wire over to the east."

"The south wire would be even more conve-nient for them," commented Brant.

"Mebbe the cows were bunched better and closer over to the east," returned Webb.

The subject was dropped, but Brant still re-mained thoughtful.

Brant continually patrolled the Running W range, but without tangible results. The same applied to his line riders. And still the spread continued to lose cattle. Brant took to riding far to the west, near and past the borders of the Running W holdings. One day found him near where spurs of the craggy hills of New Mexico encroached on the level plains of the Panhandle. He was riding slowly, his keen eyes sweeping the terrain on all sides, when he noticed a group of moving blobs appear from a bristle of thicket to the north. He quickly identified them as half a dozen riders forging steadily in his direction. He watched them for a moment, then glanced around. His eyes narrowed as he spotted a second group of riders to the south and somewhat behind him. The direction of their progress, if maintained, would meet them with the group from the north at approximately the spot where he himself sat his tall moros.

His black brows drawing together, he spoke to Smoke and sent him forward at a fast clip. Instantly the two groups altered direction slightly. As he progressed, he still remained the focal point of the converging horsemen.

"Thought so," he muttered, speaking to Smoke again. "Looks like those gents sort of want to be sociable. A mite too sociable, the chances are."

His diagnosis was confirmed a moment later. A puff of whitish smoke mushroomed up from the group to the north. Before the crack of the distant rifle reached his ears, a slug whined past in front of him.

"Gettin' playful, eh?" he exclaimed. "Reckon I'm in for some fun. Trail, Smoke, trail!"

Instantly the great moros shot forward, his speed increasing at each beat of his irons. Brant, cooly watching the hard riding horsemen on either side, saw other puffs rise from their ranks. Bullets whined past.

Brant was not particularly concerned. The distance was too great for anything like accurate shooting. Barring the chance of a freak shot, there was little danger of the slugs reaching their mark. And he was confident that Smoke's great speed and endurance would soon put him beyond reach of the pursuit. He glanced ahead. The hills were close now, the track he was following leading up their lower slopes to a dark notch into which it flowed. It was nothing more than a game trail, Brant decided, but the going was good.

"Won't take us long to lose those *amigos* in the rocks up there," he assured the moros. "Then we'll circle south and get back to our range. Lucky there's a way up the hill. If they got us hemmed in along the base of those sags, they'd corner us in a hurry. Reckon that's what they figured on doing. Must have been keeping an eye on us for quite a spell. Good things we wern't farther to the south. That crack up there looks to be about the only way out."

Smoke was slowly drawing away from the pursuers. Breathing easily he mounted the long slope and flashed into the notch. The game trail had petered out, but the going between the frowning cliffs was still good. Soon the cliffs to the north fell away. Brant found himself riding on a narrow shelf that ran west with a southward veering. On his right was a sheer drop of hundreds of feet. To the left was a steep brush grown slope that extended for perhaps a hundred yards, ending at the base of a granite wall that fanged upward into the blue. The southward trend of the shelf tended to a constant curving. At no place could he see more than a few hundred feet in advance.

The shelf became broken and uneven, also littered with loose boulders. Brant was forced to slacken Smoke's pace. He kept glancing over his shoulder.

"Don't want those hellions to get within good shooting range of us," he muttered, "that is if they're still on our tail."

The shelf straightened out. For nearly a quarter of a mile it ran directly westward, until a bulge of cliff, around which it curved, obscured its continuation. Brant had covered perhaps two thirds of the distance to the bend when, on glancing back, he saw a string of horsemen bulge around the last curve behind him and come thundering down the straight-away.

"Gained some on us," he told himself. "Well, they can't make any better going here than we can, and they're still too far back to have much luck throwing lead."

He reached the bend, sending Smoke careening around the bulge. Again the shelf straightened out for a short distance. From Brant's lips burst an exasperated oath.

What had been a rather exhilarating race suddenly became something deadly serious. Directly ahead, less than two hundred yards distant, a crack in the cliff wall cut across the shelf. A gulf of unknown depth yawned between where the shelf ended and where it resumed on the far side. And the gulf was better than twenty feet in width!

Automatically, Brant's grip tightened on the reins. But he instantly realized that to pull up would be as fatal as to plunge into the chasm ahead. His brain worked at lightning speed. On one side was the sheer drop into nothingness. On the other, above the slope, the cliffs shot up sheer. There was no place to go but ahead. And ahead yawned that pitiless gulf.

Brant made his decision. His voice rang out; urgent, compelling—

"Trail, Smoke, trail! Sift sand, you jughead, it isn't a very good take-off, but you'd ought to be able to make it."

He breathed a sigh of thanksgiving that he was riding the moros today, instead of some other critter from his string. A lesser horse would never be able to clear the gap and land safely on the continuation of the narrow shelf, which he realized now was several feet lower than the point of take-off.

Smoke snorted protest, but he laid his ears back, extended himself and drummed the rock with flying irons. Straight for the lip of the chasm he charged, pouring his long body over the ground. He squealed with apprehension as he gathered himself together and launched out over space. Brant had a hair raising glimpse of the tops of pine trees below, like to waving feathers in the depths. Then Smoke's front irons clanged on the cracked and fissured rock beyond the gap. He lurched wildly as one hind foot failed to find solid ground beneath it, scrambled, lunged, keeping his balance by a miracle of agility. Brant eased off on the reins, abruptly realizing that sweat was pouring down his face and that his pulses were pounding.

"That one was close!" he gasped as Smoke flashed down a straight stretch that continued for some hundreds of yards. He whirled in the saddle as shots clanged behind him.

The pursuit, driving their foaming horses at top speed, has rounded the bend above the gap. Their yells came to Brant's ears. In a fleeting glimpse he noted that the riders were masked. Another moment and Smoke was swerving around a bend and out of sight. The whoops of the pursuers grew faint as the wall of rock shut them off.

But there was something disquieting about those shouts. It seemed to Brant they held a note of triumph, of mocking derision.

"What in blazes they got to holler about?" he asked himself. "I'm willing to bet a hatful of pesos not one of those hellions will chance taking that jump. And with a horse that hasn't got what it takes like Smoke has, a jigger would be plumb loco to try it."

Smoke rounded the bend ahead and Brant abruptly understood. He pulled the moros to a halt, staring ahead.

"No wonder those hellions were whooping it up!" he exclaimed. "I'm trapped!"

Chapter Twelve

Hooking one leg over the saddle horn, he rolled a cigarette and considered his predicament. The shelf continued for something like a hundred yards, gradually narrowing until it petered out altogether. On one side was a gorge hundreds of feet in depth. On the other, above the narrow slope, sheer cliffs shot upward for other hundreds of feet. Ahead was dizzy nothingness. It would be impossible for Smoke to negotiate the gap behind, with the going up hill and taking-off point considerably lower than the far edge of the gulf more than twenty feet distant.

Brant's gaze roamed about. Smoke, he decided, could make out very well for a while. The slope from the shelf to the base of the cliffs was grass grown. In several places he had noted trickles of water. But Brant could not subsist on grass, like Nebuchadnezzar. He faced either a quick death by hurling himself into the gorge, or a slow one by starvation. He pinched out the butt of his cigarette, turned Smoke and rode slowly back toward the gap, eyeing the slope on his right the while. He rounded the final turn with caution, although he had little fear that the owlhoots would be waiting for him.

"They wouldn't hang around," he told Smoke. "Wouldn't figure they had to, and they'd want to get in the clear as quickly as possible. Chances are they headed us through the notch in the hills on purpose—had it all figured out and knew that if we didn't go down that crack when you tried to jump it, they'd have us hogtied just the same. Uh-huh, either I would pull up at the gap in the ledge and shoot it out, or would try to make you jump it. They didn't care whether you made the jump or not. Well, this will take a mite of thinking out."

The owlhoots were nowhere in sight as Brant approached the gap. He rather wished they were holed up around the turn on the far side and loosened his Winchester in anticipation. They would have to show themselves to take a shot at him, and he grimly decided if they did, at least one or two would remain on the shelf to keep him company. But the ledge lay silent and deserted.

Brant leaned over and peered into the gorge. It was fully as deep as the canyon on his left. The walls were sheer, impossible to descend. He shook his head, studying the ground at his feet. The shelf was seamed and cracked, with deep crevices several inches in width scoring its surface.

"Mighty lucky you didn't stick a foot into one of those cracks when you landed," he told Smoke. "You'd have gotten a busted leg sure as shooting."

He measured the distance across the gap with his eye, shaking his head. He had already considered the possibility of dropping some sort of a bridge over the fissure, but his survey told him there were no trees growing there above twenty- or twenty-five feet. No trunk that would bear his weight was available. He fingered the rope slung to his saddle. It was sixty feet in length, twice the length needed to span the fissure, but there was nothing on the far side over which to drop a loop. The situation appeared more hopeless the longer he considered it. He rolled a cigarette and smoked thoughtfully, racking his brain for some solution to the problem. Absently he unlooped the rope and swung it back and forth in his hand. Abruptly he uttered an exclamation. A leaping light glowed in his eyes.

"Feller," he told Smoke, "I believe I've got a notion, and I believe it will work. If it doesn't, there's nothing lost."

He studied the crevices in the surface of the shelf, deciding on two that he figured would suit his purpose. Then he turned the moros and rode slowly back along the shelf, scanning the slope above.

"Those are a couple right up there that had ought to do," he told Smoke, measuring two stout saplings with his glance. The little trees coasted trunks that ran straight and fairly thick for better than twenty feet.

"Cut 'em down, lop off a few branches, and I figure they'll do," he decided.

Dismounting, he clambered up the slope to where the saplings stood. Surveying the trunks, he drew his heavy pocket knife and opened the blade. Then he shook his head.

"It would take a week to gnaw 'em down with this sticker," he muttered. "Calc'late I know a better way."

He pocketed the knife, stepped back and drew his gun. He emptied all six chambers at the trunk, spacing the bullets across its thickness. The heavy slugs did not quite dust both sides of the tree, but Brant knew they came pretty near to doing so. He reloaded, emptying the gun again. Stepping around the tree, he repeated the operation from the other side. As he continued to fire, the tree shook and swayed and began to lean slightly down the slope. Brant holstered his gun, reached up as high as he could and caught the trunk with both hands, swaying down with all his weight. The weakened tree leaned more and more. With a sharp snapping sound, the trunk broke off where it had been almost severed by the bullets from Brant's Colt.

"One!" he exclaimed, and went to work on the second sapling. With both trees lying on the slope, he carefully trimmed away the branches, leaving a short length of a stout limb near the upper end of each trunk. Then he tumbled the logs down the slope and dragged them to the edge of the gap. He took his rope and tied one end to the stub of the limb he had left near the smaller end of the sapling. He performed a like service with the other end of the rope on the second trunk. Then, with considerable difficulty, he raised one of the saplings to a vertical position and wedged the end securely in a crevice near the lip of the gap, securing it with small boulders jammed and hammered into the crevice. The second sapling went into position in a second crevice some three feet to the right of the first. Brant stood back and eyed his handiwork with satisfaction.

The two trunks stood straight and firm. Dangling between them was a swing formed by the loop of the rope secured to the stubs near the tops of the two uprights.

Brant got the rig off Smoke and piled it at the base of the slope. "Well, feller, here we go," he told the moros. "If I make it, I'll come back and get you pronto. If I don't, well I'll wait for you on the 'other side' of the Big Jump."

He drew the looped rope back and stepped into the loop, thrusting out strongly with one foot as he drew it up. The swing swayed out over the gap.

Brant began to pump as a boy does in a swing when he has no one to push him. Back and forth he swung, gaining height and distance with each sway of the noosed rope. Finally he was covering more than half the space across the gap at each outward swing. The saplings creaked and groaned, swaying and bending under his weight. With a cold finality, Brant realized what would happen if one should break or become dislodged. Far beneath, the feathery tops of the pines swayed in the draft that soughed down the crevice, revealing the black fangs of stone between which they grew.

Back and forth. Back and forth. Brant realized that he was reaching the apex of the inverted arc and was as near the far edge as he could hope to be. He measured the distance to the lip as it rushed toward him, set his teeth, tensed his muscles, and leaped forward with all his strength.

As he rushed through the air with hundreds of feet of nothingness beneath him, for one horrible instant he was sure he had jumped short. Then his boots thudded on the very crumbling lip of the bench. Frantically he hurled himself forward. He hit the stone with a shock that knocked the breath from his body. For a moment he lay half stunned, waves of blackness sweeping over him.

Then, gasping and panting, he sat up, shaking in every limb, his body bathed in a cold sweat, but with a wild exhilaration pounding his pulses. He staggered to his feet, waving a hand to the watching horse. His voice rang out in triumph—

"Made it, feller! Made it! You take it easy. I'll be back for you."

He chuckled as he started on the long trudge to the ranchhouse. "Somebody is sure going to be sold!" he told himself exultantly.

Brant had little doubt as to who was responsible for the attempt on his life. He immediately discounted the New Mexico outlaws.

"Those hellions wouldn't have taken the trouble to wear masks," he reasoned. "Every jigger of them already has a price on his head and the noosed end of a rope waiting for him. Being implicated in another killing wouldn't bother them. Nope, I reckon my *amigos*, Doran and Hansen, were out to even up the score. But I've a prime notion they wouldn't be taking such a chance just to pay me off for bustin' up Doran there in the Deadfall. Nope, there's more to it than that. Those sidewinders have something to cover up—something they're afraid I'll catch onto if I'm left maverickin' around. But in the name of blazes, what?"

Dawn of the following day was breaking when Brant, footsore and deathly weary, limped up to the Running W casa. Without arousing anybody, he tumbled into bed and within a few minutes was sound asleep. When he awakened, around toward noon, he felt little the worse for his harrowing experience. His first thought was the rescue of his horse from the bench.

This was accomplished with little difficulty. A light wagon loaded with long and stout planks toiled up the slope and rumbled through the notch in the hills. Riding attendance were Brant and half a dozen punchers. The planks were dropped over the crevice and Smoke was led across, lifting his hoofs gingerly and snorting as the boards swayed and bent beneath his weight.

"You better stop ridin' around by yourself," John Webb cautioned his foreman. "Always have some of the boys with you. The hellions are out to get you, and they won't stop. Luck was with you this time, but next time they may do a better job of stackin' the cards."

Brant, however, chose to disregard the well-meant advice. He felt he had a much better chance of running a brand on the wide-loopers if he played a lone hand. He continued to ride the range. But now he employed a different method. Instead of searching the brakes and the thickets and scanning the prairie from vantage points, he continually swept the sky with his keen gaze. Finally, one crystal-clear afternoon, he spotted what he had been searching for. Rising from behind a straggling grove was a thin streamer of smoke.

Brant cleared the distance between him and the grove at a gallop. He raced around the edge of the growth, sliding his Winchester from the saddle boot. As he cleared the last fringe of brush, he viewed what he had expected to see. Crouched beside a small fire were two men. A cow lay on the ground nearby, roped and tied.

The men sprang erect as the low thunder of

Smoke's irons smote their ears. One waved his hat in a circle. The other held a rifle in his hands.

Without slackening speed, Brant charged toward them. The man threw the rifle to his shoulder. At the same time, Brant cuddled his cheek against the stock of his Winchester.

The two shots rang out almost as one. A bullet fanned Brant's face. The rifle wielder hurtled backward as if struck by a giant fist, and fell. His companion, crouched behind the body of the prostrate cow, was shooting with both hands. A slug nicked Brant's shoulder. A second burned the skin of his neck. His own gun boomed sullenly. The cow jerked and twitched, stiffened out. Brant shifted his aim the merest trifle and squeezed the stock. The brand blotter slumped sideways. When Smoke foamed up to the fire, he was as motionless and as satisfactorily dead as was his companion.

Brant dismounted. He peered closely at the faces of the two men and shook his head. Both were hard featured characters, and both were unfamiliar to him. He turned his attention to the cow. It also was dead, drilled squarely between the eyes. Brant uttered an exclamation as his glance fell upon the brand.

"Hell!" he muttered, "it isn't a Running W critter. It's one of Norman Kane's Flying V's!"

The stench of scorched hair and flesh assailed his nostrils. He bent over the brand, touched the seared flesh with a tentative forefinger. Suddenly his eyes widened. He bent closer. A moment later he whistled softly through his teeth. He rocked back on his heels, staring.

"Well, I'll be darned!" he muttered at length.

He straightened up, swept the surrounding terrain with a searching glance.

"Got to make sure about this," he muttered. "If I'm right—well—"

He left the sentence uncompleted, turned and examined the nearby growth with his eyes. He picked up one of the dead brand blotters and carried the body into the thick growth. Returning, he performed a like office for the second man. Then he turned his attention to the two well-trained horses that, despite the shooting, still tautened the ropes noosing the dead cow. Taking their rigs off Brant turned them loose. Each bore an almost undecipherable brand, more like a skillet of snakes than anything else.

"Mexican burn," Brant muttered. "Practically impossible to tie up with anything."

He concealed the rigs in the brush, then noosed the cow's neck hard and fast to his pommel.

"All right, feller," he told Smoke. "You got a chore to do."

With little difficulty, the powerful moros dragged the body into the grove. Brant drew his knife and went to work. With care, he cut out the section of hide upon whch the brand was burned. He ripped it loose, turned it over and examined the inner side. Again he whistled, his eyes glowing.

"I was right," he muttered, "plumb right. Now I understand where our cows have been going. Of all the slick schemes, this is the limit! Darn nigh foolproof, too. If the hellions hadn't gotten so nervy and took to doing their blotting in broad daylight, the chances are we never would have caught on. Now to get the evidence on that hellion. This isn't enough. He'd like as not win out in a court fight. Well, I reckon it's up to me. Got to play a lone hand. Isn't right to ask anybody else to take chances."

Brant left the dead cow and went to work cutting brush. He piled the cut branches over the body of the cow and the bodies of the dead brand blotters. Nor did he neglect the two rigs he removed from the horses. Within an hour he had all the evidence of the recent happening thoroughly concealed. He uprooted boulders and weighted down the heap of brush, against the chance of coyotes rooting out the bodies. He speculated the two horses that were quietly grazing nearby.

"Would be taking too much of a chance to lead them away," he decided. "Let 'em run loose. If they drift back home, it'll puzzle the hellions, and mebbe scare 'em a mite, but I don't think they'll tie 'em up with what happened. Not soon enough to do them any good, anyhow."

Mounting Smoke, he rode swiftly for home. Twilight was falling when he reached the ranchhouse. He ate his supper, talked with Webb for a while and then retired to his room in the casa, ostensibly to sleep. But as soon as things were quiet, he slipped out again. In the tool shed he selected a pair of heavy wire cutters.

"Here's where I become a law breaker," he muttered. "Got a feeling it's justified, though. No other way I can figure to get the lowdown on that sidewinder. Taking a chance, but there's no way out that I can see."

Saddling Smoke, he rode south by west again. The night was dark and silent when he approached the wire that enclosed Norman Kane's Flying V spread. He rode slowly along the fence, peering and listening. Finally he reached a spot where a number of cattle were bunched. He drew rein and dismounted.

Brant knew he was taking a chance. If Kane's riders happened to be patrolling the fence and sighted him, he could expect no mercy. And there was the disquieting thought that an overlooked shotgun bomb might be planted somewhere in the vicinity, although he rather doubted it. He had a feeling the fence was not being patrolled. If he was right in his suspicions of the Flying V owner, he was sure it was not. But there was the catch. He might be all wrong in his surmise. And if he was, and Kane was vigilantly guarding his wire, John Webb would likely need a new foreman tomorrow.

Leaving Smoke standing with dangling reins, Brant approached the fence. The grazing longhorns raised heads and eyed him suspiciously. He could see the starlight glinting on their rolling eyes. Some snorted and moved farther from the fence. An old bull rumbled deep in his throat, as if considering the advisability of a charge. Brant set the cutters against the top wire.

The snip-snip of the tool sounded loud in the stillness. Brant paused a moment. The night remained silent. He went to work again, cutting the strands from top to bottom. He moved to the next post and repeated the performance. The wire fell to the ground, leaving a wide gap in the fence. Nothing else happened. Brant slipped back to his horse, expectantly.

Shadowy and grotesque in the wan starlight, the cows began moving toward the gap, following an instinct that seems inherent in all cattle.

Brant watched them stream through. He turned Smoke and rode back the way he had come, pushing the moros as hard as was advisable. He realized he had no time to waste.

Chapter Thirteen

The Running W hands didn't take kindly to being roused from their slumbers in the dark hours before the dawn, but a few words of explanation shot them wide awake and rarin' to go. They saddled up in a jiffy and thundered south by west toward the cut in Norman Kane's wire.

It was already full of daylight when they sighted the Flying V fence. A number of cows had streamed through the gap and were scattered about on the Running W range. The cowboys rode among them, peering at brands with shrewd experienced eyes. Finally Brant singled out four critters for special examination. These were herded together and headed for the Running W casa.

"We got to june along," Brant told his men. "If we got caught down here, there'll be some prime gun slinging before we're ready for it; and if I've slipped up in this business, we'll find ourselves on a mighty hot spot."

Old John Webb was in the ranchhouse yard when the troop arrived, driving the protesting cows before them. He let out a bellow of astonishment.

"So you work dodgers have decided to go in for a little wideloopin' for a change, eh?" he roared.

"You take them Flyin' V cows right back where they belong! What's the big notion, anyhow?"

"They're not Flying V cows, Uncle John, they're Running W cows," Brant grinned as he dismounted.

Old John glared at him. "So!" he rumbled. "I always figgered you'd crack up sooner or later—too darn much book larnin'!' Runnin' W cows! I can't trust my own eyesight, I suppose?"

"Not this time you can't," Brant chuckled. He turned to his men.

"It's a shame to have to cash in the poor critters, but there's no help for it," he said. "Okay, shoot 'em and get the hides off."

While the astounded Webb looked on speechless, the order was obeyed. Soon four green hides were stretched on the ground, hairy side down. Brant silently pointed to the "evidence."

All of the four cattle chosen by Brant were young steers, none much beyond the calf stage. An experienced cowman knows the brand on a calf is written plainly inside the skin; one burned on later is less definite, and, if the animal is getting old, is sometimes not visible at all. Courts recognize the validity of the testimony of experienced range men concerning the markings on a dried hide.

And on the four green skins stretched before his eyes, John Webb saw the indubitable marking of the earlier burned Running W brand!

Webb, his eyes literally starting from his head, turned to Brant in bewilderment.

"Who—what—how—" he sputtered.

"One of the slickest jobs of brand blotting I ever saw, that's all," the foreman returned. "Don't you see how it was done? Half of a Running W, with a little altering of the horizontal bars, is just about the same as a Flying V. Remember when we met Norman Kane the first time that day up at Doran's Crossing. You remarked to him that your burn, the Running W, started like this but was twice over. A pretty good description of the Running W when set against the Flying V. Now recollect how Kane's branding iron is shaped. On each side of the letter is a flat 'ear.' When the brand is stamped on the hide, the burn left is just like this—"

Brant stooped and traced the mark in the dust at his feet.

"See it? Okay. Now blot half of the Running W, set the V carefully over the other half and the flat ear completely effaces the blot. Then just a mite of work with a running iron—a cinch ring or a piece of telegraph wire would do the trick—and there's a perfect Flying V. After a few days, not even a careful examination on the outside of the hide, would show that the brand had been altered. But yesterday, I ran onto those two blotters just as they were finishing their chore. Even then, if they hadn't given the game away by waving me 'round, I doubt if I would have caught on. They could have said they were just branding an unmarked critter they had reason to believe belonged to their outfit. It was only after I leaned down close to examine the brand that I caught on. They worked a mite fast and hadn't quite covered the blotted half of the W as they would have if they hadn't been interrupted."

"How about the ear-marks?" asked Webb.

"Another thing that worked out prime for

Kane," Brant replied. "Our ear-mark is an under-split. His is an under-bit."

Brant again drew a diagram in the dust. "Two swipes with a knife blade and the change is made. You'll notice the ear-marks on these hides are fresh cut."

Old John's face set in lines hard as chiselled granite. "Okay," he said, "wait till I get the rig on my horse. We'll ride down there and clean out that nest of sidewinders."

But Brant instantly vetoed the proposition. "No," he said, "we won't. We'll take care of this matter in a law abiding way, so that there will be no comeback. We'll take these hides to the sheriff at Tascosa and lay our evidence on the boards. We've got all we need. There'll be plenty of cows on Kane's range with altered brands. I counted nearly a dozen besides these four in that bunch I turned out last night. We've got Kane up against a stacked deck. The sheriff will deputize us to assist him. We'll catch them flat-footed and I figure there won't even be any resistance, which will all be to the good. No sense in getting somebody plugged or cashed in when we don't have to. We'll do this right."

"Reckon you're talkin' sense, per usual," Webb admitted. "Okay, let's head for town. Pack up them hides and bring 'em along."

In Tascosa, Sheriff Willingham grimly examined the four hides. "It's an open-and-shut case," he said. "We'll ride down there and take 'em in. I'll swear in you fellers as a sheriff's posse. We'd oughta catch 'em flatfooted, and I figger we won't have a mite of trouble."

However, the sheriff was considerably wrong in his "figgerin'." Just then one of the Running W cowhands hurried in.

"Boss," he said to Brant, "them two jiggers what own the Posthole—Doran and Hansen—just rode out of town skalleyhootin'. They forded the river and headed south by west. Sure were foggin' the dust. I figgered you'd oughta know about it."

Brant instantly swung into action. "Those two hellions are in cahoots with Kane, of that I'm sure," he told Willingham. "They've caught on, somehow, to why we're here. They're headed down there to warn Kane and the bunch. If we don't get right on their tail, the whole lot of them will slide across into New Mexico."

"Let's go!" barked the sheriff.

Five minutes later the posse thundered out of town, with excited citizens thronging the streets. The waters of the river boiled to foam as they stormed through the shallows. Then with irons drumming the hard surface of the trail, they raced south by west. At the crest of each rise they stared anxiously ahead, but many miles were covered before they sighted Doran and Hansen pushing their horses up a long slope.

"They got a head start, but we're gainin' on 'em," grunted the sheriff.

Brant nodded, estimating the distance yet to go and the lead the hard riding pair enjoyed. For a moment, confident in Smoke's great speed and endurance, he contemplated pushing on ahead of the posse, but reluctantly dismissed the notion. He knew Sheriff Willingham would not approve.

Also, he had nothing definite on Doran and Hansen that would justify slinging lead at them, and he knew that if he came within rifle range, a gun fight would be inevitable.

Mile after mile they travelled, the horses wet with sweat, their nostrils flaring, and their breath sobbing and panting.

"If those hellions down there have time to fork their bronks, we're done," Brant told himself. "Our cayuses are going to be just about finished by the time we make the Flying V."

But before the Flying V wire came into sight, Brant's pulses were pounding with exultation. Doran and Hansen were now within long rifle range, and their lead was being cut down by the minute. Plainly, their mounts were giving out. Less than six hundred yards separated pursuers and pursued when the pair swerved their staggering horses through the gate and flung themselves out of their saddles in front of the Flying V ranchhouse. From the crest of a rise, the posse could see figures running wildly about; but when they had negotiated the far side of the sag and again sighted the casa, not a man was in sight. The house itself lay ominously quiet, with closed door and shuttered windows.

Sheriff Willingham halted his troop just outside gunshot range. "They're holed up in there, all right," he said. "Okay, you fellers wait here. I'll ride ahead and have a pow-wow with 'em."

"I'll ride with you," Brant offered.

"No you won't," the sheriff declined emphatically. "You'll stay right where you are. If those hellions are out to get anybody, it's you. I figger they'll hardly take a shot at me alone. Wouldn't gain 'em anything but a murder charge which, so far as I know, there isn't, yet."

He rode slowly forward, his badge of office gleaming on the front of his sagging vest. A few yards from the gate he reined in.

"Norman Kane!" he shouted.

For a moment there was silence, then Kane's clear voice replied:

"Well, what is it?"

"I have a warrant for you, Kane," the sheriff called back.

"Okay, come ahead and serve it, if you figger it's healthy," Kane's voice jeered.

Willingham moved his horse forward a pace. A rifle cracked inside the house. A bullet whistled past the sheriff's head.

"The next one won't miss," Kane warned.

The sheriff reined in his horse. "You can't get away with it, Kane," he shouted. "If you won't come peaceably, you'll come anyhow."

"Mebbe," Kane replied, "but I figger we'll thin out your bunch considerable before you bust in."

"Okay," the sheriff answered quietly. "You've asked for it, now you'll get it."

With this ultimatum, he wheeled his horse and rode back to the waiting posse.

"Get that fence down and ride in," he ordered. "We can slide up purty close to the house through the brush. Four men work around to the back. Must be a back door to that casa. Don't let 'em slip out that way. Okay, let's go."

Ropes were flipped to the tops of fence posts, a section of the wire was razed. The possemen rode through, dismounted and tethered their horses in a thicket. Then they began to creep forward, taking advantage of all cover that offered. A shot rang out, another and another. Bullets whined past, clipping leaves and twigs.

"Got loopholes between the logs," the sheriff grunted. "Must have figgered on somethin' like this from the start." He glanced at the sun. It was low in the west.

"Not long till dark," he said. "That's what they're playin' for—time. They figger they can slide out once it gets real dark, and give us the slip. All right, you fellers, see if you can do something to slow up that gun slingin' before somebody gets hurt."

The possemen opened fire, aiming at the chinks between the logs. The fire was returned from the ranchhouse. Sheriff Willingham swore angrily.

"We're just about as close as we can hope to get," he told Brant. "And it ain't close enough. If we try to rush 'em, across that open space, we're goin' to lose men, and there's no guarantee we can bust in even if some of us make it to the door. The hellions wouldn't neglect that angle. Them planks look thick, and chances are they're double or triple with iron bars across 'em."

Brant was studying the ranchhouse. "I got a notion," he exclaimed suddenly. "Be back in a mite, Cape."

Brant began working his way back through the brush. In the thicket where the horses were tethered he paused. He located a tough withe which he cut and trimmed. He notched the ends, fumbled a bit of string from his saddle pouch, bent the stave and strung it. He had a fairly serviceable bow. Three more slender withes provided arrows which he trimmed with care, weighting one end of each with a bit of stone wedged in a notch. He removed his neckerchief, tearing it into three strips. These he dampened slightly at a trickle of water nearby. Then, with his teeth, he wrenched the bullets from several cartridges. He sprinkled the powder over the slightly damp cloths and rubbed it into the fabric. He spread the cloth in a patch of sunlight and let it dry for a few minutes. Then he carefully wrapped a strip around the head of each arrow. With this contraption under his arm, he made his way back to the sheriff. The possemen were still keeping up a desultory fire, which was answered from the casa. The uneasy whine of passing lead punctuated the reports.

"What in blazes?" demanded the sheriff as Brant crouched down beside him.

"The Indians used to do it," Brant chuckled. "If they could, I don't see why we can't."

The sheriff understood instantly. "Fire arrows!" he exclaimed. "By gosh, I've a notion it would work, if you could drop one onto the roof. Those roof boards and shingles are dry as tinder; they'd oughta burn easy. But son, you couldn't ever shoot an arrow onto the roof from here with that thing."

"I know it," Brant conceded. "But do you see that big boulder over past that string of bushes? If I was behind that rock I could do it easy."

"Uh-huh," agreed the sheriff, "but you ain't there, and a mighty slim chance of gettin' there with them hellions in the house watchin' every move. You'd be plugged before you got half way to that rock."

"Mebbe," Brant conceded, "but I figure it's

worth riskin'. Pass the word to the boys to cut loose with everything they got on those chinks. Some of 'em are bound to put a slug or two through, and with lead whizzing around 'em, I've a notion those gents in the house won't be up to their best at shooting."

"You're taking one awful chance, but okay," the sheriff agreed dubiously. "May save a heap of shootin' later on, and I reckon it's about our only chance to bag the lot of 'em. Go to it!"

The word was passed along and the possemen redoubled their fire. Slugs pounded the logs. Brant saw dust and clay fly from the chinks between the logs in several places. With the firing at its height, he slipped from behind his shelter and ran at top speed for the boulder, bending almost double, weaving and zig-zagging. He had covered more than half the distance when the owlhoots in the house discovered him.

A slug ripped his shirt sleeve. Two more, striking almost together, whisked his hat from his head. Another struck the heel of his boot and nearly knocked him off his feet. Still another drew blood from his scalp and the shock rendered him weak and dizzy for a moment. With a headlong dive he reached the shelter of the boulder and crouched behind it, trying to regain his breath. Then he carefully fitted an arrow to the string of his bow, struck a match and applied it to the powder smeared rug.

The rag burned fiercely, snapping and sputtering. Brant raised the bow, drew the arrow to the head and let go. It described a flaming arc through the air and dropped squarely onto the roof. Two more fire arrows followed as swiftly as

Brant could light them and bend the bow. He dared not lift his head to see if his ruse was successful, but a moment later the exultant whoops of his companions assured him that it was. Another moment and he could see the cloud of smoke that billowed up from the flaming roof.

"Get set!" Sheriff Willingham's voice rang above the din of the shooting. "They'll be bulgin' outa there in a minute. The roof's already darn nigh to fallin' in. Look at her crackle!"

Brant drew his guns, every nerve tingling, every sense at hair-trigger. He could see the flames now, boiling up from the fiercely blazing roof. The air was thick with smoke and the pungent whiff of burning wood. The roar of the fire dimmed the cracking of the guns.

"Here they come!" boomed the sheriff.

Brant leaped to his feet. The besieged defenders were streaming out the front door, shooting as they came. Foremost were Phil Doran and Pink Hansen.

Both Brant's guns let loose with a rattling crash. Doran reeled backward and fell, his guns dropping from his nerveless hands. Hansen, his face a mask of hate and baffled fury, took deliberate aim at Brant. Brant pulled trigger at the same instant. A lock of black hair spun from the side of his head as his Colt bucked in his hand. Through the fog he saw Hansen spin around like a top, slew sideways and fall. Guns were cracking on all sides. Brant saw three of the owlhoots go down, two like crumpled sacks of old clothes, the third kicking and clawing in the dust. Then he was abruptly aware that the firing had ceased. As the smoke cleared, he saw five men standing in front of the burning ranchhouse, their hands raised high. They were bawling for mercy.

"How's it goin' in back?" bellowed the sheriff.

"We've got two here," came the answer. "That's all that came out this way."

"Is one of them Kane?" Brant shouted.

"Nope, ain't seen him," was the reply.

"Must be inside burnin' up," put in the sheriff. "He ain't here in front."

Brant thought differently. He bounded around the corner of the ranchhouse, and swore in exasperation. In the north end wall of the casa a section of a log had been removed, leaving an opening wide enough for a slender man to wriggle through. Even as Brant glanced about, a pounding of hoofs sounded.

"There he goes!" roared Sheriff Willingham as Norman Kane's tall bay flashed across an open space between two thickets.

Brant raced to his horse, flung himself into the hull and sent Smoke crashing in pursuit.

Kane was heading north by west, hoping undoubtedly to reach the hills and the New Mexico line. Brant knew, however, that he would have to ride some miles northward before an opening in the hills would provide him a line of escape. He sent Smoke forward at top speed, veering to the left the while, so as to get between Kane and the hills. It was tough going through the brush and the heavier and more powerful moros gained on the bay. Brant could see Kane glancing back from time to time, his face a white blur. He still rode north, edging westward the while, but soon it became apparent to both that he could never make the hills and safety before his pursuer came up with him. Abruptly he altered direction, heading the bay east for the near wire that enclosed his land.

Brant saw the bay take the wire, soaring over the strand like a bird. He sent Smoke charging after him. Smoke cleared the wire with no difficulty. But now the open prairie was before them and the bay, bearing the lighter load, held his own. Try as he would, Brant could not close the gap between them. He fingered the stock of his rifle and shook his head. The distance was too great for anything like accurate shooting from the back of a racing horse. To use the Winchester, he would have to slow up, which would give the fugitive a chance to widen the distance between them.

"And it'll be dark soon now," Brant muttered. "Let him get a mite more ahead of me and he'll give me the slip once the night really shuts down. Can't be at all sure of downing him at this range, and in this light. Nope, we've got to run it out."

He settled himself in the saddle and concentrated on getting the last hoof-beat of speed out of the flying moros.

Smoke responded nobly, but the bay held his own, even drew away a trifle. Brant's face set in bleak lines. Kane was gradually veering to the south. Once let him lose his pursuer and, under cover of darkness, he could circle west to the hills and safety.

And then abruptly Brant saw something less than a mile ahead, something that he recognized. Barring the path of his quarry was a long, irregular crack in the level prairie. It was a canyon, one of the many offshoots of the Palo Duro. It was indeed little more than a crack, compared to the great gorge into which it emptied, but nevertheless it was more than thirty feet in width with perpendicular walls dropping down to the rocky floor hundreds of feet below.

A moment later Kane sighted the widening gorge. Brant saw him rise in his stirrups and survey it coolly, then settle himself back in the hull and urge his mount to greater speed.

"Blazes!" Brant muttered. "He's going to try and jump it! He can't do it, at least I don't figure he can. Smoke might make it, but I don't believe that bay can. Trail, feller, trail! We got to try to stop him!"

Snorting, blowing, slugging his head above the bit, the great moros extended himself to the utmost. Eyes rolling red, his glorious black mane tossing in the wind of his passing, he gave his all in one final glorious burst of speed. Swiftly he closed the gap between him and the flying bay.

But now the ominous gorge was close. Dusk was falling and the deep gulf was brimful of shadows. Brant saw Kane gather up his reins, ram his feet deep in the stirrups. He raised his voice in a stentorian roar—

"Don't try it, Kane! Don't try it! Pull up while you can!"

Norman Kane glanced back. Brant caught the flash of his eyes. Then once more he faced to the front and sent his horse charging at the dark gulf.

The bay never faltered. On he raced. Brant saw his muscles bunch for the leap. And then, on the very brink of the gorge, he stumbled. Gallantly he strove to recover. It was too late to turn. With an almost human scream, he launched himself forward through the air.

Up and up! in a splendid curve, he shot toward the far lip of the gorge. He reached the apex of the arc while still many feet from safety. Brant's breath exhaled in a whistling gasp—

"Short!"

Norman Kane twisted in the saddle, waved a mocking hand to his pursuer and rode grandly into eternity!

Chapter Fourteen

"Went out like a man!" Brant told Webb and Sheriff Willingham. "Hard as steel and cool as a dead snake to the last. Never turned a hair as he went down that canyon. A pity that a jigger who had just about everything that goes to make a man should turn to riding a crooked trail."

"You say you'd suspected him for quite a spell?" Webb remarked.

"Yes," Brant replied, "ever since he sliced off your best range like he did. It was legal, of course, but it was a mighty sharp practice just the same. And I've noticed that a jigger who goes in for sharp practices usually won't hesitate to step across to the wrong side of the law if it fits in with his plans. Then that day we rode down to where he was building his ranchhouse, something else came to me. For quite a spell, I'd been puzzling over who in blazes could have informed Phil Doran that I was packing that dinero of yours. All of a sudden I realized it must have been Kane. He was present when the matter was discussed. That night he checked out of the hotel there in Dodge City. Of course he got ahead of me and lined Doran up. The day we found him and Cole there together, I asked him if Doran was enjoying good health when he left the Deadfall. Kane stiffened up and didn't know how to answer. I was just about certain then, and, of course, when Doran and Hansen showed up in this section and Kane went into cahoots with them in opening up the Posthole, I was plumb sure. That business of his wire always being cut on the east side was another angle. Kane cut his own wire mostly, and let his own cows drift out onto our range."

"Why?" Webb asked.

Brant chuckled. "That was pretty smooth," he replied. "You'll recollect Kane 'lowed some of his critters might still be maverickin' around loose, after we'd rounded up all we could find? And you'll remember, too, every now and then the boys would find a few more sliding around in the brush? Those were our cows, with the brands altered from Running W to Flying V. Our boys were plumb obliging and herded 'em right over to Kane. I've a notion he got quite a laugh out of that caper."

"The nervy sidewinder!" Webb growled.

"By the way," Brant asked, "did you find Cole Dawson cashed in?"

"Dawson's gone," replied Webb. "I learned from our prisoners that he rode off several weeks ago and never come back."

"Glad to hear it," said Brant. "For all his pigheadedness, I figure Dawson was an honest hombre. I reckon when he caught on to what Kane was pulling, he couldn't abide it and trailed his rope. Chances are we'll never see or hear tell of him again."

"That won't make me feel bad," grunted Webb.

Two days later, Brant rode to the Bar O ranchhouse. "Webb is taking me in with him as a partner," he told Verna Loring. "I've talked him into breeding better stock, fencing his range and getting ready for the time when the cattle boom is going to bust and it'll be hard going for any cowman who is caught with his twine tangled. Webb agrees I'm right but says he's too old to make the changes by myself and that it's up to me to carry on for him. We shook hands on it.

"Reckon I'm in business for myself from now on. Feel sort of expansive. I'd build me a ranchhouse for myself in the grove over east of the Running W casa if I could just get somebody to help me look after it."

Verna glanced up demurely through the silken veil of her long lashes.

"Why, Austin," she said, "I wouldn't want you not to have your new ranchhouse!"

Some time later, old Nate entered the room and shook his grizzled head in mock disapproval.

"Son," he chuckled, "it looks to me like you done got yourself hawgtied!"

"When you think of the West, you think of Zane Grey." —*American Cowboy*

ZANE GREY

THE RESTORED, FULL-LENGTH NOVEL, IN PAPERBACK FOR THE FIRST TIME!

The Great Trek

Sterl Hazelton is no stranger to trouble. But the shooting that made him an outlaw was one he didn't do. Though it was his cousin who pulled the trigger, Sterl took the blame, and now he has to leave the country if he wants to stay healthy. Sterl and his loyal friend, Red Krehl, set out for the greatest adventure of their lives, signing on for a cattle drive across the vast northern desert of Australia to the gold fields of the Kimberley Mountains. But it seems no matter where Sterl goes, trouble is bound to follow!

"Grey stands alone in a class untouched by others." —*Tombstone Epitaph*

ISBN 13: 978-0-8439-6062-4

FIRST TIME IN PRINT!

OUTLAWS
PAUL BAGDON

Spur Award Finalist and Author of
Deserter and *Bronc Man*

Pound Taylor has just escaped from jail—and the hangman's noose—and he's eager to get back on the outlaw trail. For his gang he chooses his former cellmate and the father and brothers of his old partner, Zeb Stone. Pound wants to do things right, with lots of planning and minimum gunplay, but the Stone boys figure they can shoot first and worry about the repercussions later. Sure enough, that's just what they do—and they kill a man in the process. With the law breathing down their necks and the whole gang at one another's throats, Pound can see that hangman's noose getting closer all the time. Unless his friends kill him first!

ISBN 13: 978-0-8439-6073-0

ROBERT J. CONLEY

FIRST TIME IN PRINT!

No Need for a Gunfighter

"One of the most underrated and overlooked writers of our time, as well as the most skilled."
—Don Coldsmith, Author of the Spanish Bit Saga

BARJACK VS...EVERYBODY!

The town of Asininity didn't think they needed a tough-as-nails former gunfighter for a lawman anymore, so they tried—as nicely as they could—to fire Barjack. But Barjack likes the job, and he's not about to move on. With the dirt he knows about some pretty influential folks, there's no way he's leaving until he's damn good and ready. So it looks like it's the town versus the marshal in a fight to the finish... and neither side is going to play by the rules!

Conley is "in the ranks of N. Scott Momaday, Louise Erdrich, James Welch or W. P. Kinsella."
—*The Fort Worth Star-Telegram*

ISBN 13: 978-0-8439-6077-8

John D. Nesbitt

"John Nesbitt knows working cowboys and ranch life well enough for you to chew the dirt with his characters."
—*True West*

FIRST TIME IN PRINT!

Will Dryden picked the wrong time to ride onto the Redstone Ranch. He was looking for a job...and a missing man. But one of the Redstone's hands was just found killed, so tensions are riding high and not everyone's eager to welcome a stranger. The more questions Dryden asks, the more twisted everything seems, and the more certain he is that someone's got something to hide. Something worth killing for. Dryden just has to make sure he doesn't catch a bullet before he finds out what's behind all the...

TROUBLE AT THE REDSTONE

ISBN 13: 978-0-8439-6055-6

LOUIS L'AMOUR

For millions of readers, the name Louis L'Amour is synonymous with the excitement of the Old West. But for too long, many of these tales have only been available in revised, altered versions, often very different from their original form. Here, collected together in paperback for the first time, are four of L'Amour's finest stories, all carefully restored to their initial magazine publication versions.

BIG MEDICINE

This collection includes L'Amour's wonderful short novel *Showdown on the Hogback*, an unforgettable story of ranchers uniting to fight back against the company that's trying to drive them off their land. "Big Medicine" pits a lone prospector against a band of nine Apaches. In "Trail to Pie Town," a man has to get out of town fast after a gunfight leaves his opponent dead on a saloon floor. And the title character in "McQueen of the Tumbling K" is out for revenge after gunmen ambush him and leave him to die.

ISBN 13: 978-0-8439-6068-6

The Classic Film Collection

The Searchers by Alan LeMay

Hailed as one of the greatest American films, *The Searchers*, directed by John Ford and starring John Wayne, has had a direct influence on the works of Martin Scorsese, Steven Spielberg, and many others. Its gorgeous cinematic scope and deeply nuanced characters have proven timeless. And now available for the first time in decades is the powerful novel that inspired this iconic movie. (Coming February 2009!)

Destry Rides Again by Max Brand

Made in 1939, the Golden Year of Hollywood, *Destry Rides Again* helped launch Jimmy Stewart's career and made Marlene Dietrich an American icon. Now available for the first time in decades is the novel that inspired this much-loved movie. (Coming March 2009!)

The Man from Laramie by T. T. Flynn

In its original publication, *The Man from Laramie* had more than half a million copies in print. Shortly thereafter, it became one of the most recognized of the Anthony Mann/Jimmy Stewart collaborations, known for darker films with morally complex characters. Now the novel upon which this classic movie was based is once again available—for the first time in more than fifty years. (Coming April 2009!)

The Unforgiven by Alan LeMay

In this epic American novel, which served as the basis for the classic film directed by John Huston and starring Burt Lancaster and Audrey Hepburn, a family is torn apart when an old enemy starts a vicious rumor that sets the range aflame. Don't miss the powerful novel that inspired the film the *Motion Picture Herald* calls "an absorbing and compelling drama of epic proportions." (Coming May 2009!)

✂ ☐ **YES!**

Sign me up for the Leisure Western Book Club and send my FREE BOOKS! If I choose to stay in the club, I will pay only $14.00* each month, a savings of $9.96!

NAME: _____

ADDRESS: _____

TELEPHONE: _____

EMAIL: _____

☐ I want to pay by credit card.

☐ VISA   ☐ MasterCard   ☐ DISCOVER

ACCOUNT #: _____

EXPIRATION DATE: _____

SIGNATURE: _____

Mail this page along with $2.00 shipping and handling to:
Leisure Western Book Club
PO Box 6640
Wayne, PA 19087
Or fax (must include credit card information) to:
610-995-9274

You can also sign up online at **www.dorchesterpub.com**.
*Plus $2.00 for shipping. Offer open to residents of the U.S. and Canada only.
Canadian residents please call 1-800-481-9191 for pricing information.
If under 18, a parent or guardian must sign. Terms, prices and conditions subject to change. Subscription subject to acceptance. Dorchester Publishing reserves the right to reject any order or cancel any subscription.